That First Summer: Part One

ENCHANTED MOUNTAINS series

~

Eleanor Romany

That First Summer: Part One
Book Two of the *Enchanted Mountains* series
Cover designed using Canva
Copy editing provided by Cindy Long and Nancy Wohl
Published by Eleanor Romany
ISBN (print): 9798241803955
First Edition
Published in the
United States of America
10 9 8 7 6 5 4 3 2 1

Other books in the
ENCHANTED MOUNTAINS series

Longing for More

That First Summer: Part One

ENCHANTED MOUNTAINS series

Summer 1999

Chapter 1

Allen Kirkland slowly drove his Buick LeSabre onto the gravel parking lot of Twin Pines State Park's swimming pool, or, as locals affectionately called it, "the park pool."

The car was several years old; he bought it just before the family moved to Olmstead, New York, ten months ago. Allen liked its power windows, something he'd never had. He also liked the fact that it didn't have rust anywhere on it. Not yet, at least.

He'd let his sixteen-year-old daughter, Jonie, name the car, and she had chosen Buttercup as a joke. Jonie didn't think her father would go for it, but he called her bluff and accepted her suggestion.

Now, Allen winced as Buttercup's undercarriage scraped against the gravel.

"Yikes," Jonie said, her blue eyes opening wide as she glanced over at her father. "That didn't sound very good."

"After today, I might be dropping you off at the entrance to the park, and you can hitch a ride in with a ranger." Allen chuckled nervously as he pulled up to the pool entrance.

For decades, Twin Pines State Park had drawn visitors into its peaceful wilderness, offering sweeping views and a quiet kind of magic. Families returned summer after summer, chasing adventure and the comfort of something familiar, where nature always waited to welcome them back.

The park pool sat in the middle of Twin Pines, next to the campground where visitors either pitched tents for a rustic experience or parked their RVs for a little more comfort. Each summer, from the emerging heat of Memorial Day until the breeze began to cool with the coming Labor Day, families made going to the pool part of their summer park experience, along with hiking, biking, and stargazing.

Jonie rolled down the window. Morning air, still cool from the lake, spilled in, mixed with the scents of chlorine, fresh-cut grass, and the faint coconutty sweetness of sunscreen that always lingered.

The pool hadn't opened yet for the day. A lawnmower buzzed somewhere near the campground. Birds chirped from the pine trees that ringed the back fence, and Jonie could hear the echo of someone dragging a lawn chair into place.

Beyond the parking lot, she could see the water shimmering pale blue and undisturbed. The diving board stood still in the morning light, casting a long shadow across the surface of the deep end.

Jonie tucked her long auburn hair behind her ear and took a deep breath. Her stomach fluttered with butterflies.

It was her first day of work at the park pool.

"Tell me again. How did you get a job at a pool and you don't even know how to swim?"

"Daaaaad." Jonie rolled her eyes and looked at her watch. "I don't want to be late. I don't think Ms. Livingston would appreciate that."

"You did tell her you don't know how to swim, right?"

"Dad!"

"Break a leg," Allen said, smiling. "What time did you say to pick you up?"

"My shift ends at four."

Jonie slammed the car door closed and walked toward the entrance, her stomach tumbling with nerves. At this point, she didn't know if the butterflies were because of her new job—her first job, *ever*—or if it was the anticipation of seeing Brandon Murphy.

Brandon was the cutest guy in her junior class at Olmstead High School. He and Jonie shared a homeroom, and every morning she slinked to her seat with her eyes drilling a hole in the floor, too shy to even look his way.

One morning, Jonie overheard him talking to his friends about his job as a lifeguard. That wasn't the whole reason she'd gotten a job at the most popular summer hangout in town, although it certainly made the idea more appealing.

Jonie stood still on the sidewalk, facing the pool. She breathed in and out deeply, trying to calm her nerves. She hadn't thought her interview with Alice Livingston, the manager of the park pool, had gone well. Then two days later, the telephone rang at her house. When her mother answered it and told her it was a call for her from Ms. Livingston, she couldn't believe it.

"Okay, here we go," Jonie said quietly under her breath as she walked through the turnstile entrance of the pool. "Whatever you do, don't drown."

Jonie knew she was lucky to be able to spend her summer at Twin Pines State Park. Especially because she had applied for jobs at fast food restaurants, the movie theater, and even a salon. She didn't know the first thing about flipping burgers, the movie theater was always too cold, and she didn't think she could be very happy sweeping up hair all summer.

Ms. Livingston's voice suddenly rang out from the intercom.

"Please report to the gazebo for our morning huddle."

Jonie was startled; she hadn't even had a moment to get her bearings. She hoisted her tote bag higher on her shoulder and looked around. She had planned on stuffing it into a locker, but now she didn't have time.

Employees from across the pool stopped what they were doing and headed toward the huddle. Jonie hadn't noticed a gazebo during the small tour she went on during her interview, so she quickly fell into step behind a guy with black hair and a red hoodie sweatshirt who seemed like he knew where he was going.

As she walked quickly, Jonie rummaged through her bag. She tried grabbing a pencil as it rolled around.

"Dang it!" She peered inside the bag, and just as she grabbed the pencil, she suddenly slammed into something hard.

"Ouch!" Jonie looked up as the young man in front of her stumbled forward, his hands catching himself just before he fell all the way down. He quickly stood up straight and whirled around.

It was Brandon.

"Hey, what was that for?" he said, his eyebrows knitted in confusion as he rubbed his hands together to get rid of the wet speckles of freshly mowed grass sticking to them. He looked down to check his sweatshirt, the one he always wore that had "Olmstead High School Tigers Basketball: Class of 2001" on the front.

"I'm so sorry!" Jonie's face turned a deep crimson. She could feel her cheekbone start to ache. "You have a hard shoulder."

Brandon grinned, his brown eyes twinkling, as he flexed his right arm. "Yeah, I've got quite a bit of muscle going on."

"Very funny." Jonie was sort of smiling inside, but the side of her face hurt so much she couldn't make it actually happen. Besides, this wasn't the way she wanted to start her new job and *definitely* not the way she wanted to start her new job where the boy she sort of liked worked, too.

Brandon examined Jonie's cheekbone and then glanced toward the gazebo.

"You're going to be fine. We don't want to be late. Here, give me that." He grabbed Jonie's bag from off her shoulder, lifted it onto his, and began walking quickly toward the gazebo. "Good grief, what the heck do you have in this thing?"

Brandon reached the gazebo five steps ahead of Jonie.

"Wait!" she exclaimed as he plopped her bag onto the wet grass. Jonie groaned, imagining all the little green stains on the bag she'd bought especially for this job. She picked it up and pulled out her notebook and pencil. Then she stood and focused her attention on Ms. Livingston, who was standing on the top step of the gazebo.

Jonie felt completely flustered. She looked at her watch. She hadn't even been at work thirty minutes.

It's going to be a long day, she thought.

~

Alice Livingston stood inside her office at the park pool and watched her newest employee, Jonie Kirkland, get out of a car and wave goodbye to a man Alice assumed was her father. Actually, Alice had no doubt the two were related: Jonie's stick-straight auburn hair matched the color of the man's hair, and deep dimples appeared on both of their smiling faces.

She glanced at her watch. It was seven-thirty in the morning, about two hours before the pool opened. There was always so much work to be done before opening each day: vacuuming away leaves and bugs that had fallen into the water overnight; checking chemical levels; arranging deck chairs and loungers.

Alice didn't think anyone understood just how much work went into making sure the pool was perfect each day.

She sighed and massaged the bridge of her nose. She'd woken up with a slight headache and wanted to get rid of it before it got worse. Glancing at the empty Mr. Coffee four-cup drip pot, she decided there was time to make more before she brought everyone together for the morning meeting.

Half an hour later, Alice locked the office door behind her and slipped the key into the front pocket of her khaki shorts. The familiar scent of damp pine needles and just-mowed grass met her immediately. She paused a moment at the top of the sidewalk that led to the Olympic-sized pool and let the morning settle around her. A woodpecker knocked methodically from somewhere near the campground, and a crow called back like they were keeping each other in check.

The cracked sidewalk leading toward the gazebo was still shaded, and her sneakers made soft scuffing sounds on the concrete. To her right, the pool sat quiet and blue, the surface glassy under the morning light. Alice knew someone had skimmed it already, but pinecones had dropped in since, floating gently near the deep end. She made a mental note to fish them out after the huddle.

In the mornings, Twin Pines State Park smelled earthy and sun-warmed, with a hint of chlorine and campfire smoke drifting in from last night's embers at the nearby campground. Alice passed a picnic table where a squirrel froze mid-chew, eyeing her warily before darting away.

When she reached the gazebo, she rested her hand briefly on one of its wooden posts. The paint had started to peel again. She remembered when her father built the railing himself, muttering about splinters and warped boards but smiling the whole time. Her mother had planted marigolds around the perimeter. That first summer the pool opened, Alice had helped serve lemonade to guests right here, and it had been a magical time for the sixteen-year-old.

Now, Alice looked out at the pool, the lifeguard chairs, the hills rolling gently behind them, and the first hints of bright sunlight slipping between the pines. Thirty-five summers had flown by. Her parents were long gone now, and so much had changed. So much except the steadfastness of Twin Pines and the pool.

Alice took one more breath, then turned to greet her staff.

Twenty-five individuals, mostly teenagers and young adults, packed tightly around the gazebo. They all had notepads and pencils, and they looked up at Alice, waiting for her to give instructions and thoughts for the day.

"Good morning, everyone. According to Tony Captiva on Channel 3 News, it's going to be another hot day. No rain, no clouds."

Alice always began her morning huddle with a weather report. Although most mornings, like this one, everyone could already tell how hot it was going to be. Some staff members were already wiping sweat from their foreheads and fanning themselves with their notebooks. Brandon Murphy lifted his sweatshirt over his head and tossed it over his shoulder. Alice wondered why he wore the sweatshirt at all; but he did, everyday.

"I would like to introduce a new staff member we have for the summer." She looked at Jonie, who was standing next to Brandon. The left side of Jonie's face was very red; Alice didn't recall noticing that when she first saw her this morning. She made a note to herself to ask about it later. "This is Jonie Kirkland."

Everyone turned to look. Jonie gave a feeble wave and smiled.

"Hey everyone." Her voice cracked with nervousness, and she cleared her throat. "I'm happy to be here."

"Jonie will be my assistant this summer. That means if you need anything, she can help you." Alice paused. "She won't be in the water, though. We have enough lifeguards for that. She's here to help us with anything on land."

Alice smiled softly at Jonie. She'd already decided that no one needed to know Jonie couldn't swim. Sure, it was an out-of-the-ordinary thing to do—hire someone who couldn't swim to work at a swimming pool—but that wasn't really a necessary skill for the assistant job. Besides, Alice hadn't known how to swim when her parents first opened the pool decades ago. In fact, she'd learned when she was around Jonie's age.

"Let's go through the big events of the day, and then we'll all get to work," Alice continued. "Today is Thursday, so that means the kids from Tiny Trails Daycare Center will be here from ten until around one. I've talked to the center's director about the trash the kids have been leaving behind. But if it doesn't get picked up, Sarah and Mark, please make sure you get that done as soon as they leave."

A few daycare centers around town loved bringing their kids to the pool during the summer, and Alice was generally happy to oblige, even though sometimes it meant a lot of extra work.

"The other big event today is that we have a birthday party starting at three." A quiet groan moved through the crowd, and Alice laughed a little to herself. "I know, I know. Jonie, we'll need your help here. Let's get together after the huddle and go over the details."

Alice watched Jonie scribble something down. She also noticed Brandon watching her. He'd barely been able to take his eyes off of her during the entire meeting, but Jonie hadn't seemed to notice.

"Okay, everyone, huddle is over," Alice said. "Let me know if you have any questions." She looked at her watch. "We have about an hour and a half before the doors open. Oh, and Christopher, can we make sure to display the small bags of pretzels today on the counter in the concession stand? We ordered too many, and we really need to get rid of them before they expire."

"We could sell them two for fifty cents," Christopher replied.

"Good idea. Thank you."

Alice watched Christopher head away from the gazebo along with the rest of the team.

Chapter 2

Jonie lifted her bag onto her shoulder and looked around. Brandon was gone; he'd disappeared as soon as Ms. Livingston told them the meeting was over.

He must have a lot of work to do, Jonie thought. *Probably lifts weights before the pool opens.* She laughed, wincing at the pain in her cheekbone.

Then she felt a gentle hand on her shoulder.

"Jonie, come with me to my office," Ms. Livingston said. "Let's get you started this morning."

"Sounds good, thank you, Ms. Livingston." As they walked, Jonie half expected her to say, "You can call me Alice," but that never came.

As Jonie tried not to worry about whether or not her deodorant would hold up against all the sweating she was already doing, her mind went back to her interview.

She hadn't known what to expect from Ms. Livingston; the woman had sort of a reputation around town. Not a bad reputation, exactly, but people talked about her because she was quiet and mostly kept to herself, which made her mysterious.

Ms. Livingston reached into the zippered pocket of her khaki shorts and pulled out a heavy keyring. Jonie watched as she easily selected the key to her office without looking. She followed Ms. Livingston inside, and just as she had during her interview, Jonie sat down in one of the chairs in front of the desk and placed her belongings in the other.

"Before we begin," Ms. Livingston said as she sat down at her desk and pulled her chair forward. "What in the world is wrong with your face? Did you come to work like that?"

Jonie's hand flew to her cheek. The part of her face that wasn't red from running into Brandon turned crimson from embarrassment.

"Oh, it was nothing." Jonie felt flustered. "I wasn't paying attention earlier, and as I was walking toward the gazebo, I ran into the back of Brandon."

"I see. You have to be careful. There's so much going on here all the time, and everyone stays busy running from one area to another. Safety is always our top priority."

"Yes, ma'am." Jonie wanted to crawl under a rock.

"Like I said a few moments ago, our procedure is a little different on the days that daycare centers come," Ms. Livingston continued. "Today, with the Tiny Trails kids here, that means probably around forty kids all together." Alice paused while Jonie scribbled some notes.

"I'd like for you to observe the check-in process when the daycare gets here. It helps us determine how many hotdogs and drinks we need to have ready at noon, and you can help with that, too."

"Hotdogs ready at noon..." Jonie wrote, and she drew a big star beside the note to indicate its importance. After she finished writing, Jonie looked up. Ms. Livingston was staring at a calendar on the wall above her desk, then snapped her attention back to Jonie.

"When we're done here, please spend the morning with Jennifer Lehman, she'll teach you how to handle everything."

"Okay, sounds good. Should I find you after I help with the daycare center check in?"

"Yes. There's plenty more for you to get started on." The telephone in the office began to ring, and Jonie hurriedly gathered her things. She gently closed the door as Ms. Livingston reached for the receiver.

Outside the office, she let out a slow, deep breath. Before she went looking for Jennifer, she decided she needed a moment to herself.

Thankfully, the women's locker room was empty. Its fluorescent lights were bright, and black flies buzzed around, trapped inside. The cinder block walls were painted a lilac purple, and along one wall were white lockers, the same kind Jonie used in high school.

She walked to the row of white porcelain sinks and peered at herself in the mirror. Her cheek looked a little puffy from where she ran into Brandon's shoulder, but it wasn't as bad as she expected.

Suddenly, the door swung open and a girl wearing the same hunter green polo Jonie was wearing walked in, hairbrush in hand. She shook her blonde hair out from her long ponytail and smiled at Jonie before looking at herself in the mirror.

"Hi, I'm Jennifer Lehman. You're the new assistant, right?"

"Yeah! I'm Jonie Kirkland."

"Welcome to the park pool! Where the lifeguards are hot, the hotdogs are not, and the fun never ends."

Jonie laughed. She liked Jennifer immediately.

"Ms. Livingston said for me to hang out with you this morning while you check in the daycare kids. I hope that's okay."

"Totally fine." Jennifer held a rubber band between her teeth as she twisted her hair into a messy bun on top of her head. "I'm happy to have company that isn't hyper six-year-olds."

"Just let me know how I can help," Jonie said as they walked out of the women's locker room and back into the sunlight.

"Just watch and learn," Jennifer smiled. "And don't get run over by a stampede of kids!"

~

Alice hung up the telephone and sighed with relief. It had been her doctor.

She'd been feeling tired lately, more winded walking toward the gazebo for the morning huddles and needing to pause when she climbed the stairs to the restaurant on the second floor of Twin Pines Lodge. Luckily, her fatigue was only caused by low iron.

"After fifty years, I guess I need to learn to like spinach," she laughed as she left her office and stopped by the women's locker room.

As Alice washed her hands, she felt a lightness she hadn't felt in a few weeks. She stared absentmindedly at herself in the mirror. Her ash-blonde hair was cut short, the ends barely touching her shoulders. It had always been thin, and cutting it short was the only way to give it any volume.

Alice dried her hands and shook her head a little. *Time to focus*, she thought. The pool was scheduled to open soon, and she needed to do her final walk-around to make sure everything was in tip-top shape.

~

"Glad to see you didn't drown!"

Late that afternoon, as the sun shone high and bright, Allen turned to look at his daughter as she opened the back car door and tossed her belongings on the floor behind the passenger's seat.

"Thanks," Jonie said sarcastically. She dropped into the front seat and slammed the door shut. "Good grief, Dad, can't we get the air conditioner in this thing fixed? Do you know how hot it is?"

"I do know. I've been working out in this kind of heat for, gosh, twenty years? This is just your first day."

"Yeah, yeah, I know." Jonie laughed and rolled her eyes. "Point taken."

Both were quiet as Allen maneuvered the Buick out of the parking lot at just the right angle and just the right speed. When the car didn't make a scraping sound, Allen shook his fist high in victory.

"I knew it wouldn't take me and ol' Buttercup long to get the hang of that."

Twin Pines Lodge stood majestically on the hillside above the lake, which was filled with kayakers. The shoreline was dotted with families fishing and couples snuggled together on blankets.

"Here's an idea," Allen said after a while. "Maybe you can use some of that money you're making this summer to get the air conditioning fixed."

Jonie laughed. "I might be able to do that after I pay mom back for all the stuff she let me get at the mall last weekend."

"Oh yeah, I heard about that."

Jonie was quiet for another moment and then looked over at her dad.

"Or I could save my money and buy my own car."

Allen nodded approvingly. "And you could drive your old dad around town! You could be the one to take me to work instead of the other way around. I like it."

Jonie looked out the window, feeling exhausted. The evergreens whizzed by, and she watched woodchucks dart across the park's lawns and then disappear into the brush.

Twin Pines State Park was only a twenty-minute drive from Jonie's house, but it was just enough time for her to close her eyes and instantly fall asleep. The sound of the garage door opening woke her up, and she felt disoriented and even more tired than before as she walked inside the house.

Later that evening, as the family prepared dinner, Jonie's mom, Nancy, yelled out, her head halfway in the oven.

"What was Alice Livingston like? I've heard so much about her. I can't wait to find out if any of it's true."

Jonie sat down at the dining room table.

"Mom, we've lived in this town for less than a year, and you already know all the gossip about Ms. Livingston?"

Allen brought dishes of mashed potatoes and green beans to the table and placed them beside the macaroni and cheese and dinner rolls. Jonie's mouth watered; all she wanted to do was grab a roll, swipe it through the macaroni and cheese, and then stuff the whole thing into her mouth.

"While we're at work, your mother spends all her time making friends with the town gossips," Allen said with a wink.

"I heard that!" Nancy walked into the dining room carrying a Dutch oven of meatloaf. "I just so happen to meet a lot of people during my shifts at the public library. Some of them *might* like to gossip."

"I'm starving!" Jonie said as the smell of dinner overwhelmed her senses. She couldn't remember ever being so hungry or so tired.

Once her parents were seated, Jonie began to eat. A few moments went by before she noticed the silence in the room. She looked up at her mom and dad, who were both staring at her, their forks suspended in midair.

"Wow," Allen said. "Would you like a shovel instead of that fork?"

Jonie laughed so hard she couldn't talk for a few minutes.

"I'm sorry! I can't help it! I'm so hungry, today was so busy. I didn't expect it to be that way...I didn't know what to expect."

"It sounds like Mrs. Livingston is quite the supervisor," Allen said.

"It's *Ms.* Livingston," his wife corrected him. "Jonie, what's she like? Does she really have fifteen cats living in her house?"

"Her house? I didn't go to her house. Besides, I think she just lives in her office. They say she has a cot in the back that she uses instead of a bed."

"I heard that rumor, too!" Nancy exclaimed.

"Mom, I'm just kidding." Jonie felt annoyed. Usually she enjoyed gossiping about people they met around town just as much as her mother did, but for some reason, tonight she felt protective of her new boss.

Nancy didn't seem to notice.

"My friend, Florence, said that if you ask Ms. Livingston if she's ever been married, she'll tell you no, but then Florence says she really was, many years ago. But she doesn't like talking about it."

"What happened to her husband?" Allen asked between bites of mashed potatoes.

"*Alleged* husband," Jonie interjected, glaring at both of her parents. "Who's Florence?"

"Heather Mathis' mom," Nancy replied.

Jonie rolled her eyes. Now she knew where Heather, one of her classmates, got her big mouth. If Heather wasn't talking to one of her cheerleader friends, she was talking to Brandon, and that was enough for Jonie not to like her.

"Ms. Livingston seems nice enough," Jonie said. "She's pretty private. She keeps her office locked all the time." Instantly, Jonie regretted giving her parents even a little nugget of information that might lead to more speculation.

"Ooo, I heard that, too!" Nancy said. "Someone told me that she keeps all her cash locked up in there. That she doesn't even have a bank account. All the money that pool has ever made over the years is locked up in boxes in that office." She shook her head from side to side as she reached for the meatloaf.

"I don't know," Allen said. "When I dropped Jonie off this morning, I pulled up right out front, and I saw her office. It looks pretty small. It probably wouldn't hold many boxes."

"Well, you're probably right, dear."

Jonie sighed. Then she remembered something real she had learned about Ms. Livingston.

"I meant to tell you this, Dad! During my interview, she asked me why we had moved to Olmstead, and I told her it was because of your work. She asked what work you were in, and when I told her you were a boilermaker, she said her dad had been one, too."

"Well, I'll be darned!" Allen's eyes lit up. He was proud of his line of work, even though the family moved often in order for him to be close to his jobs. It was how they'd ended up in Olmstead ten months ago and various other towns over the years to which Jonie didn't bother getting attached.

"She asked me if we moved around a lot, and I laughed and said yes. I tried to count how many schools I'd been in since second grade, and I lost count."

Jonie's father looked sad for just a moment. Then his face changed, and he looked as if he was pondering something.

"I *have* heard that the pool used to be run by her parents, and after they passed away, she took it over."

Jonie shrugged. She had no idea, and honestly, she didn't really care. Aside from telling her that their fathers were in the same profession, Ms. Livingston hadn't revealed any other information. In fact, she had seemed embarrassed that she'd told Jonie that much.

The grandfather clock in the living room rang out seven times.

"I'm really tired," Jonie said once it stopped chiming. "Good dinner, you all." She pushed back her chair and took her dishes to the kitchen.

A few minutes later, Jonie flopped down on her bed. Before she was able to get back up and change into pajamas, she was fast asleep. And she didn't move until her alarm clock went off the next morning. For the next two weeks, that would become her nightly routine.

~

The restaurant at Twin Pines Lodge was quieter than usual. It had just opened that summer, and it proved to be a big hit with both park visitors and locals. Tonight, though, the last of the weeklong campers had gone home, and a hush settled over the park.

Alice stepped inside, brushing a few pine needles from her sleeve. The scent of coffee and bread filled her senses. A few regulars sat at the heavy, wooden tables: rangers in uniforms, the park naturalist with her ever-present field notebook, and Sally, a new waitress who already seemed to know everything about everyone.

"Evening, Alice," Sally called, sliding a laminated menu onto the table as Alice sat down. "You're late. I was about to send out a search party."

Alice smiled faintly and took a seat. "I got stuck at the pool. The pump's being temperamental again."

Sally poured a glass of iced tea and leaned in, lowering her voice a little. "You'll never guess who was in for lunch."

Alice raised an eyebrow. "If this is another one of your wildlife riddles, I'm too tired to play."

"Councilman Jerry London," Sally said, her grin widening. "He sat right there by the window. Had the trout special and asked how you've been."

Alice stiffened, her fingers tracing the condensation on the glass. "Did he now."

"He said he might stop by the pool one of these days and see how the place is holding up."

Alice let out a quiet snort. "He means he's going to check if it's falling apart yet so he can swoop in with an offer."

Sally chuckled. "If you ask me, there's a little more than business behind all that interest. Weren't you always at each other's throats in high school? What do they say about people who secretly like each other?"

Alice gave her a look that could have frozen the lake outside. Sally was probably ten years younger than her; how did she know anything about her and Jerry from high school?

"We tolerated each other. His father was the one always trying to buy the pool from my parents."

"Mm-hmm," Sally mumbled, clearly unconvinced. "Still, funny how he keeps finding reasons to come around after all these years."

Alice shook her head but couldn't quite hide the curve at the corner of her mouth. "He's persistent. Some habits die hard."

Sally wandered off to refill a ranger's coffee, and for a moment, Alice's gaze drifted to the empty table Sally had pointed out. A memory flashed quickly: she and Jerry were both seventeen, and he was leaning over the fence to tease her while she skimmed leaves from the pool. He'd called her "Pool Queen" back then, and she'd sworn to push him in one day when she got the chance.

The memory almost made her smile.

Sally returned, eyeing her curiously. "What's that look?"

"Nothing," Alice said quickly, reaching for her tea. "Just remembering." Sally smirked but didn't press.

Alice took another sip of her iced tea and looked out the big picture window toward the twilight spilling over the pines. Somewhere down the hill, she could just make out the shimmer of the pool lights that should be going out soon.

"Either way," she said out loud, even though no one was around. "He's wasting his time."

But the small, thoughtful frown that lingered on her face suggested she wasn't as certain as she sounded.

Chapter 3

The black alarm clock with bright red numbers blared its usual six-in-the-morning wakeup call. Alice groaned as she slapped the snooze button. She didn't normally do that, but today she couldn't help herself.

Fifteen minutes later, she stood up from her bed and stretched her arms high above her head. Then she placed her feet into her beige fleece-covered slippers and wrapped herself in a light-pink cotton bathrobe. She didn't need to wear the robe; no one else was there. She supposed it was old habit from when she and her parents had shared the cabin.

Tucked just beyond the fence line of the park pool, Alice's cabin sat beneath a wide pine, its weathered siding the same green as the cabins peppered all over Twin Pines State Park where visitors stayed. A line of potted herbs sat along the front porch rail, and wind chimes clinked softly from a crooked nail near the door.

For decades, Alice's family had held the lease on Twin Pines' swimming pool. In the 1960s, when the state of New York wanted amenities to draw more visitors to state parks, her parents signed a concession agreement: the land belonged to the park, but the pool itself was theirs to build and run.

Every chair, every umbrella, every bag of chips in the concession stand they had paid for, maintained, and loved into place. It wasn't just park property to Alice. It was her family's legacy.

Sometimes Alice still marveled at how her life had turned out. Until she was sixteen, her family had packed up and moved every couple of years, following her father's boilermaker jobs from state to state. Just when she made a friend or grew used to a school, it was time to leave again.

But when her parents signed the lease at Twin Pines and built the pool, everything changed. For the first time, she was rooted. Summers were no longer measured by cardboard boxes and tearful goodbyes but by the smell of chlorine and the feel of sunlight, concession stand chatter, and lifeguard whistles.

Each summer, she worked alongside her parents, watching the pool grow into one of the anchors of the park. Those years gave her a steady home and a sense of belonging she'd never known before.

Every now and then, Alice also marveled at the fact that she was *still* living here. And even though throughout the past decade or so she kept more and more to herself, there was nowhere else she'd rather be than Twin Pines.

In the kitchen, Alice turned on the soft light above the stove and started the coffee pot. While she waited for it to finish, she walked into the dark living room and sat down in her off-white armchair to begin her morning meditation.

Ten minutes later, feeling a sense of calm to start her day, Alice reached into the cabinet and pulled down a maroon coffee mug that said "Twin Pines State Park Swimming Pool Grand Opening" in white letters. It was a relic from the 1960s, sold in the lodge gift shop. It was the only mug she used; she had a whole box of them in a storage closet.

When Alice arrived at her office later that morning, she looked at her to-do list: another daycare center was visiting today; monthly meeting with the landscaping crew; inventory of concessions; and a talk with one of the lifeguards about how he needed to pay more attention to the swimmers and less attention to his girlfriend and her friends.

These teenagers and their love lives, she thought with the hint of a smile.

Also on the agenda later in the week was Jonie's two-week check-in.

Alice could tell Jonie was struggling. It wasn't that she couldn't do the work, it was just that she wasn't used to having to work so hard. Alice knew when she hired Jonie that this was her first real job, and she was going to try her best to encourage her to be more confident and strong.

As she sipped another cup of coffee, Alice thought back to a recent evening. The pool had stayed open until there were twinkling stars overhead for a birthday party with a group of rowdy ten-year-olds. Several lifeguards plus Jonie had stayed late, even after working their full shift on a day when the sun had been merciless. The line at the concession stand stretched halfway down the sidewalk, and Jonie was behind the counter looking like a deer in headlights.

"Two hotdogs, no ketchup, three Sprites, one bag of Fritos!" a mother had barked. A kid was crying because he thought his ice cream was melting too fast. Behind Jonie, the grill was smoking, and the radio someone had turned on nearby was blaring static.

Alice remembered how she'd stepped in quietly, tracking down the radio and flipping the switch to turn it off and picking up the tongs from Jonie's trembling hand.

"You've got this. Take a breath," Alice had told her calmly. "Then start again. One thing at a time."

Jonie had nodded, blinking fast, and within minutes she found her rhythm: calling out orders, handing out drinks, and eventually yelling "next!" like she'd been doing this for years.

Alice was impressed with how quickly a kind and calm word reset Jonie's panic. That was the moment Alice had known Jonie would be all right, and that she was the right person for the job.

~

Later that morning, the kids from Busy Bee Daycare arrived ten minutes early. A yellow school bus rumbled into the parking lot while Jonie and Jennifer were still dragging a plastic cooler full of Capri Sun drinks from the storage closet to the concession stand.

"Oh boy," Jennifer muttered as the bus doors squealed open. "Here we go."

Screaming kids poured out like they'd been cooped up for days. One little boy immediately began chasing another around the front of the bus. A girl with pigtails insisted she had to use the bathroom right that moment. A daycare counselor in a sun visor shouted "Two lines! Two lines!" Finally, the kids settled down enough to form something that was vaguely line-shaped.

Jonie tried to look calm and collected even though the chaos of their arrival made her feel nervous. She'd observed Jennifer before, but she hadn't helped her yet.

Jennifer, on the other hand, looked like she'd been born to handle these situations.

"Clipboard." She pushed one into Jonie's hands. "You've got the headcount sheet. I've got the wristbands."

"Got it." Jonie exhaled deeply as she clicked her pen. She was so focused on the task at hand that she didn't notice Brandon had walked over.

"Hey, ladies." Brandon smiled like he was in a commercial for teeth whitening. "I thought I'd come check out today's craziness."

Jonie's heart did that embarrassing little skip it had been doing the past two weeks whenever she was within six feet of him.

"Hey," she said, trying to sound casual. She flipped her braid off her shoulder.

Jennifer still didn't look up. "Don't you have lanes to vacuum or lives to save over at the pool?"

"Already did that this morning," Brandon said proudly, like he'd just climbed a mountain. "So… what are you guys doing?"

"We're *working*, goofball." Jennifer didn't even look up from her checklist.

Jonie raised her clipboard. "Getting ready to check in the daycare kids."

"Fun," Brandon said.

Jennifer shot Jonie a look, and she had to clamp her lips tight to keep from laughing.

"Okay, busy bees," Jennifer called, ushering the kids forward. "If your counselor calls your name, step up and get your wristband. No running, no pushing, no—hey!—stop pretending your flip-flop is a telephone, we don't have time for that!"

Jonie stood beside Jennifer and double-checked the list as the kids came through. She was just starting to get into a rhythm when Brandon reappeared.

"Hey again," he said, stuffing his hands into the pockets of his red swim trunks.

Jennifer sighed loudly. "Aren't you supposed to rotate to the deep end soon?"

"Ten minutes. Plenty of time."

Then, to Jonie's surprise, Brandon gently tapped the back of the clipboard she was holding.

"You're doing a good job," he said shyly.

Jonie stared at the spot he touched like it had been blessed by the Pope.

"Oh my gosh," Jennifer muttered under her breath. Before Jonie could respond to either of them, Brandon walked back toward the swimming pool.

When the last few kids were finally checked in, the daycare group shuffled through the turnstile and toward the picnic area by the fence. When they were out of sight, Jennifer dropped onto a bench like she'd just run a marathon.

Jonie sat beside her, tucking her hair behind her ear. "Thanks for letting me help. I know I slowed you down."

Jennifer waved her off. "You did fine. Better than fine, actually. Newbies usually cry behind the concession stand after their first daycare group."

"I thought about it."

Jennifer nudged Jonie's knee with her own. "So... Brandon."

Jonie nearly dropped her clipboard.

"What about him?"

"He was hovering. Like, a lot."

Jonie's eyes widened. "He's just being friendly. I think?"

Jennifer snorted. "Please. Brandon Murphy doesn't 'hover' for no reason. He's cute, and he knows it."

Jonie pressed her lips together, thinking. She replayed the past few weeks in her head, including all the times she'd turned around and he was suddenly there with a joke, a helpful tip about working at the pool, and one day even a few snacks from the concession stand.

She had been so flustered around him and focused on not saying something stupid that it hadn't even occurred to her that *maybe* he kept coming around because he liked her.

Jennifer watched her face carefully. "Jonie. He was flirting with you, I swear."

Jonie blinked. "You really think so?"

"Oh my gosh, yes!"

She didn't answer right away. Instead, she looked out toward the pool where Brandon had finally taken his post on the lifeguard stand. He was perched confidently, tapping his whistle against his knee, scanning the water.

He suddenly glanced in her direction and waved. Jonie's heart did that embarrassing flip all over again.

She slowly turned back to Jennifer.

"I see," she said, and they both burst out laughing.

~

"Hey, Jonie Baloney!" Brandon came up behind her a few mornings later and tugged on her braid. Jonie whipped around and glared at him.

"I told you, don't call me that!"

Ever since Jennifer said that she thought Brandon kind of liked her, Jonie had started looking at him differently. What she would have considered mean before now seemed more like awkward flirting. Even still, sometimes he was just plain annoying.

"Ms. L. is late this morn. Wonder what she's up to?" Brandon peered toward Ms. Livingston's cabin and raised his eyebrows.

"She's probably filling out a pink slip for you!" Jonie replied.

"Hey! That's not very nice." Brandon tried to reach for her hand, but she maneuvered away and started jogging toward the gazebo for the morning huddle. When Brandon ran up beside her, she darted to the other side of the group.

Once Ms. Livingston arrived, only a few minutes late, it was a quick huddle. She seemed extra diligent about making sure everyone was where they were supposed to be. Afterwards, Jonie went to the office where she was supposed to meet with Ms. Livingston for a check-in.

She was kind of dreading it. She had been working really hard; almost falling asleep at dinner every night was proof enough of that. But she also knew she wasn't exactly employee of the month.

She kept forgetting her colleagues' names and putting things back where they didn't belong. She was still trying to understand every little thing that went into running a swimming pool, and it was more than she could have imagined. Luckily, she hadn't done anything bad enough to be fired over.

Oh wait, Jonie thought. *Am I getting fired? Is that what this is?* Her stomach dropped, and she suddenly felt lightheaded. She jumped when she felt a hand on her shoulder.

"Jonie, I'm sorry I'm late," Ms. Livingston said.

Jonie's mind began to race. Would Ms. Livingston let her get her tote bag from her locker before she was forced to leave? At this point, she probably wouldn't even be able to remember the combination to her lock. Who would even pick her up? Her dad was at work, and it was her mom's day off from the library, so she was out running errands until who knows when.

This was all too much for Jonie, and she felt like she might throw up.

Inside the office, Ms. Livingston sat down, placed her elbows on the desk, and pressed her palms together, as if in prayer. She looked at Jonie without a smile. Jonie decided to do a preemptive strike.

"I've really appreciated my time here, Ms. Livingston." Her voice shook a little. "This is really just the best place in town for someone my age to work, that's what everyone at school says anyway, and so if you think this isn't going to work out, let me just grab my tote bag maybe..."

Jonie noticed a small smile tugging at the corners of Ms. Livingston's mouth.

"Did you think I was going to fire you?"

Jonie stared at her boss.

"Well, I... I mean, I thought maybe it was a possibility."

"Do you *want* me to fire you?"

"Of course not!" Jonie, shocked by the question, practically yelled.

Ms. Livingston's small smile now widened. And Jonie began to relax a little.

"The reason I wanted to talk to you today is to check in and see how you're doing. I'm glad to have you here, and I wanted to make sure that there wasn't anything I could do to make your transition easier."

Jonie started breathing normally again and wiped her sweaty palms on her shorts.

"It's not always easy coming into a new job," Ms. Livingston continued. "Your family moved here last August, right? You're still feeling like you're the new kid, sometimes, I bet."

"That's exactly how it feels!" Jonie said. "Some of the kids who work here go to my school, but they're older, so I don't know them all that well. Except for Jennifer. And Brandon. He's been pretty nice to me, for the most part."

"For the most part?"

"He's pretty goofy. He leaves silly notes in my locker once. He can be pretty annoying a lot of the time, but I like him." Jonie was looking down at her hands while she talked. When she looked up, she realized she'd basically just told Ms. Livingston that she had a crush on Brandon. She felt her face turn pink.

Ms. Livingston looked thoughtful. "Did you say that he leaves notes in your locker? He isn't allowed..."

"Oh!" Jonie laughed. "No, he doesn't come into the women's locker room. He asked another girl to run in there and put it in my locker."

Jonie tried sneaking a look at the wall clock to see how much longer she had to endure this terribly awkward conversation.

"Brandon is a good lifeguard," Ms. Livingston nodded. "I'm happy to have him helping out."

Jonie knew that Brandon thought it would be cool to own a pool. Jonie wasn't so sure, she told him. Didn't he see how stressed Ms. Livingston was all the time?

"It's important to remember what your priorities are." Ms. Livingston sounded stern. Jonie's gaze had wandered above Ms. Livingston's head, but when she heard her boss's tone, she snapped her attention back.

"Okay," she said, a little confused. "You mean my priorities here at the pool? I always have my to-do list that you give me. And I check everything off as soon as I'm finished."

"That's not exactly what I meant. Yes, you are very good at prioritizing your work here. And I appreciate it, we all do. Even though you're my assistant, you're also a big help to everyone else."

Jonie's cheeks turned pink again, but this time from a small sense of pride. That was the biggest compliment Ms. Livingston had given her. And Jonie didn't realize until that moment how much she had been craving that approval, not just from her boss but from anyone. She had stopped trying to talk about work with her parents; it seemed like all they wanted to do was gossip.

"Thank you, ma'am."

"You're welcome." Ms. Livingston paused. "I can see that you're smart and capable. I think pretty soon you'll have a lot of options in front of you, and it's important to prioritize them."

"Options like summer jobs and friends and maybe college?"

"Yes, exactly."

"Well, I do know already that I'd love to work here every summer!" Jonie suddenly felt self-conscious, afraid she was being too forward.

Ms. Livingston laughed softly.

"That's good to hear."

Jonie looked at her watch, then looked up quickly.

"What is it?" Ms. Livingston asked.

"I was supposed to meet Brandon by the gazebo a few minutes ago so he could show me how to fold and unfold those new lounge chairs that were delivered yesterday."

Ms. Livingston frowned slightly.

"Those are easy to set up. I'm sure you could do it perfectly fine on your own."

"I know, but he really wants to show me. He wants to be all manly or something." Jonie suddenly felt the energy of the room shift as Ms. Livingston stood up.

"Make it quick, then." Her tone was harsher than Jonie had ever heard it. "We don't waste time around here. The pool opens in forty-five minutes. Brandon is a lifeguard; he isn't even responsible for chairs."

"Yes, ma'am."

As Jonie headed toward the door, she was suddenly scared that she'd just ruined her entire relationship with Ms. Livingston. And that she had gotten Brandon into a lot of trouble.

~

Later that day, Jonie sat on top of a picnic table with her feet resting on the bench, enjoying her fifteen-minute afternoon break. The breeze tugged lightly at the stray pieces of hair coming loose from her French braid. She closed her eyes for a second and let the sounds settle around her: the soft bounce of a basketball from the nearby court, the distant rustle of wind moving through the pine trees, and the faint echo of children's laughter from the shallow end of the swimming pool.

Mornings at the park usually started crisp, the kind of cool that made the pool feel like a shock to the system. By the time the hot afternoon arrived, the cool water was a relief.

Everything here felt alive. The scent of pine needles and warm pavement, the shimmer of the blue water, the soft slap of flip-flops on concrete. Even the bees moved slowly, drifting from clover to clover like they were in no rush.

Jonie had never had a summer like this: rooted in one place and in a rhythm. No boxes half-packed in the hallway. No goodbyes looming at the edge of August. Just sky and sun and the steady routine of pool shifts and lunch breaks and the park holding everything in place.

As Jonie closed her eyes and tilted her face toward the sun, she heard a rustling nearby. She looked to her left and there was Brandon, squinting at her against the sun.

"Hey," she said, caught off guard.

"Hey yourself. Is this seat taken?"

As Jonie smiled and nodded her head from side to side, Brandon sat down beside her. He opened a bottle of water and took a long drink, then leaned back on his elbows, peering up at the sky.

"So..." Brandon said. Jonie glanced at him. He'd gotten tan already, just a few weeks into pool season. Jonie, on the other hand, slathered sunscreen onto her pale, freckled skin several times a day.

"What?"

"Where are *my* cheese puffs?"

Before heading to the picnic table, Jonie had grabbed her usual afternoon snack from the concession stand: a small bag of cheese puffs and a Diet Sprite.

Jonie laughed. She held the half-eaten bag of chips toward Brandon. "Here, you can have the last few."

Brandon peered inside the bag.

"It's all little pieces! That's just cheese puff powder."

"It's better than nothing."

"Easy for you to say." Brandon grabbed Jonie's can of Diet Sprite from off the table and took a swig.

"Gross! You better not be putting your mouth on that."

Brandon smiled, and a little bit of Sprite ran down the corner of his mouth. He wiped it away with the back of his hand as Jonie laughed and threw the last of her cheese puff dust at him.

"You're so gross."

"Just for you," Brandon said with a smile.

"Oh, gee, thanks!" Jonie looked at her watch. They had four minutes until they had to get back to work. She didn't mind at all; she thought Brandon had seemed kind of weird today, even for him.

"It's almost time to head back," Jonie said, as she stared up at the sky and wiped sweat from her forehead with the back of her hand.

"We still have a few minutes." Brandon stretched his tan legs out in front of him. "I've been meaning to ask you, what do you normally do on a Friday night?"

"What do *I* do on a Friday night?" Jonie wasn't sure she heard him.

"Yes, *you*."

"Sometimes my mom and I go to a movie, or we watch one at home. Sometimes we play Monopoly or card games and order pizza."

"Don't you have any friends?"

Jonie felt like the wind had been knocked out of her. She stared at the crisp green grass below her feet. When she'd first sat down at the picnic table, she had kicked off her sneakers. She suddenly wanted to leave. Her eyes scanned the grass and found her shoes, a few feet away underneath a small mulberry bush.

"I didn't mean for it to sound like that," Brandon said after a moment's pause. "You just never talk about your friends or tell any stories about them. And no one ever comes to visit you here."

"Is that allowed?" Jonie asked, eager to change the subject. "I didn't think we were allowed to see our friends while we're working."

"We're not." Brandon gave Jonie a mischievous wink. "What about Jennifer? You two are always talking and laughing."

"I think Jennifer is a work friend," Jonie said thoughtfully. The realization hit her: why *hadn't* she ever invited Jennifer over or asked her to go to the mall?

It annoyed her that Brandon was asking these questions. She looked at her watch again, and it really was time to get back to work. The last thing she needed was for Ms. Livingston to be mad at her and Brandon, especially after that strange meeting she'd had with her earlier that day. She hadn't told Brandon about it, and she probably wouldn't. Besides, she didn't really like him at that moment as much as she did earlier.

Why was everyone being so weird today? Jonie wondered.

~

It seemed like every joint in Alice's body ached when she moved. Nothing had helped that day. Was fifty *really* supposed to feel like this?

The pool closed down each evening at eight. Tonight, Alice decided she could use a slow, easy swim. The movement would be good for her, and she knew the exercise would help her sleep more soundly.

She did one final check of the property; not because she really thought she'd forgotten anything, but because she wanted to make sure everyone had left for the night. Once she was certain, she went into the women's locker room and changed into the blue-and-yellow striped one-piece she kept in her office.

For Alice, an evening swim was like her morning meditation.

The water had been warm most of the late afternoon, but as the sun started to set, it had begun to cool. She dipped her right toes in first.

"Ahhh." She turned around and, with her back to the water, slowly climbed the ladder down into the shallow end.

Alice leaned back until her hair was touching the surface, then she lifted her feet off the pool's bottom. She let her body float effortlessly, carefully stretching her arms above her head as if she were trying to reach something just behind her. She sighed, releasing her breath from deep within her.

This feels amazing, she thought.

Alice floated on her back, arms stretched out, eyes open to the night sky. Her ash-blonde hair fanned around her face, forming a crown. Every sound from the world above was muted beneath the hush of the pool: the faint hum of insects in the trees, a far-off owl calling a few times.

Above her, the sky was velvet-black and scattered with stars. The pines that lined the pool property swayed gently, their dark silhouettes framing her view like the edges of a snow globe. The pale moon was only a sliver.

Alice's body ached from the day, but here, in the water, the heaviness dissolved. She felt closest to herself in the water, especially at night when the world softened and everything quieted down.

The scent of chlorine lingered, but so did the sharper smell of damp pine and the faint sweetness of the marigolds planted along the fence line. Somewhere nearby, a frog croaked.

Alice understood why people came to the pool. She understood the healing powers of water. When people visited Twin Pines, they came to get away from something.

It was that way for her parents: they moved there almost thirty-five years ago and decided they were staying. Her mother taught second grade and her father worked at a power plant nearby for a few years before saving up enough money to build the pool.

As her parents got older, they were that adorable little couple reminding guests to put on sunscreen or handing out popsicles on an extra hot day. Alice enjoyed her job, but she wasn't the face of the pool, not like her parents were. She preferred to stay behind the scenes.

Alice stood up and moved slowly into the deep end. The air was still and so was the water, except for the ripples she made as she extended her arms out from her sides and dipped her hands under the surface.

Pretty soon, the water was up to her chin. She took a deep breath, closed her lips tight, and dove underneath.

Chapter 4

"Hey," Angie Bonpensiero said the next day as she passed by Jonie and Jennifer carrying a bucket of cleaning supplies. "Later this week, some of us are heading up to cabin twelve on Bear Ridge Trail. It's empty through the weekend. You all should come."

Angie, who had worked at the park pool for the past two summers, was mostly in charge of the locker rooms and was currently on her way to do a midday cleaning.

"Cabin twelve?" Jennifer whispered loudly as she ate her lunch next to Jonie at a picnic table. "Ooo, the forbidden cabin."

Jonie looked at them both, her eyes wide.

"What's the forbidden cabin?"

Angie sighed and set the bucket down on the picnic table, stretching her arms above her head as if it had weighed twenty pounds. She pushed her glasses up on her nose.

"Cabin twelve is at the very back of Bear Ridge Trail, all by itself. It's totally hidden in the woods. My friend has a friend who works up at the lodge, and sometimes when no one is staying there, they let me know so we can go up there."

Jonie's eyes grew even wider. "Are we allowed to do that?"

"No," Angie said, voice flat. "Obviously not. Which is why we go after work and don't tell anyone." Then she picked up the bucket of cleaning supplies and scurried off toward the locker rooms.

As they watched her walk away, Jennifer bumped Jonie's shoulder. "Come on. I've never been. Besides, Brandon's probably going."

"Oh." Jonie tried to sound casual. "Cool."

Jennifer smirked like she knew better. "And tell your parents you want to spend the night at my house. It'll be fun."

Even though Jonie felt slightly nervous about breaking into a park cabin, the bigger part of her felt exhilarated. She'd never done something like that.

Friday evening couldn't come fast enough. As closing time neared, the last of the crowd trickled out of the pool, leaving behind damp footprints, the echo of kids' laughter, and the smell of sunscreen lingering in the humid air. The sky was turning gold as the sun slid behind the ridge of pines. Brandon and a few of the other lifeguards packed away their items and straightened their areas, while Jonie and Jennifer locked up the concession stand.

Twenty minutes later, the two girls walked together along the paved path that led from the pool toward the campground. The evening was still warm, and a breeze had picked up, carrying the smell of pine needles and grill smoke from the campsites.

Off in the distance, families played cards at picnic tables, kids roasted marshmallows, and someone strummed a guitar. Cicadas buzzed overhead in the branches.

"This place is a whole different world at night," Jonie murmured in awe.

"Right?" Jennifer said. "Daytime Twin Pines is chaotic. Nighttime Twin Pines feels like a secret that only we know about."

Cabin twelve on Bear Ridge Trail was tucked deep in the woods, up a short hill where the gravel path narrowed and the trees crowded closer. An overhead light with moths dancing around it lit up the weathered porch, but inside the cabin was pitch dark. Angie, Brandon, and two other lifeguards, Mark and Kyle, were already there, gathering fallen tree branches for a fire.

"Hey!" Brandon called. "Ladies of the land crew, welcome to our illegal gathering."

Angie laughed as she tossed small branches into the firepit. "Or as I like to call it... creatively unauthorized."

Brandon grinned, then looked at Jonie. "Glad you came."

"Me too," she smiled, hoping she didn't sound as breathless as she felt.

The six of them built a small fire in the pit behind the cabin, and soon the flames crackled softly, casting warm, flickering light across everyone's faces. Someone turned on a battery-powered radio, tuned to a station playing Matchbox Twenty.

They sat on logs and old folding chairs that had been left behind from the last visitors. Jonie ended up between Jennifer and Brandon, which Jennifer noticed immediately and whispered "You're welcome" under her breath. Jonie felt her face turn a deep crimson and hoped the darkness hid it.

Mark told a story about a camper who had sneaked their cat into the swimming pool last summer. Kyle stood off to the side, trying to explain a ridiculous backflip he'd seen someone do that day. And Jennifer imitated Ms. Livingston giving one of her "be professional" speeches, complete with a pretend key ring at her hip.

Everyone howled. Jonie laughed so hard her ribs hurt. She hadn't laughed this freely in, well, she didn't know.

When the group settled and conversations broke off among pairs, Brandon nudged her knee lightly with his.

"How's the job treating you? Regretting not flipping burgers instead?"

"Absolutely," Jonie said. "I could be in the air conditioning at McDonald's right now. Instead, I smell like sunscreen and hotdog water."

"Hotdog water has a very specific scent. Not everyone can pull it off."

"Why thank you. I try."

Jennifer suddenly leaned close to her and whispered, "Jonie, we're so in. This is like... our crew now."

"Our crew?" Jonie repeated, amused.

"Yeah! I never thought I'd be sitting behind a cabin in the woods at Twin Pines with the cool kids."

Mark overheard her. "We are so not the cool kids," he said, throwing a pinecone at her.

"Speak for yourself," Angie said, flipping her hair dramatically over her shoulder. They all laughed.

The fire popped sharply. A shower of sparks floated upward and dissolved into the dark.

Jonie hugged her knees and took it all in: the laughter, the music, the smell of the fire, and Brandon's knee ever so lightly brushing hers. It hit her that when school started back, she wouldn't walk into the building alone. She'd recognize faces. She'd have people who waved at her in the halls. She'd have stories from that first summer at the park, ones she'd remember forever.

Brandon leaned a little closer, his shoulder warm against hers.

"You're coming back next summer, right?" he said quietly.

Jonie smiled at him. "If I can."

"You should. You fit in here. Everyone likes you."

"They do?"

"Yeah." He stared at the fire. "I do, too."

Jonie's breath caught in her throat. There it was, the confirmation she'd been waiting on for weeks.

Brandon totally liked her. And in that moment, she wished the summer could last forever.

Chapter 5

It was Sunday afternoon, and Jonie sat crossed-legged on her bed, half listening to the radio and half trying to read. Normally the music was blaring; she loved the band Third Eye Blind, and every time that one song came on, she belted it out.

But today, the radio was turned down. Jonie didn't want to miss the telephone ringing downstairs. On Friday, when everyone was leaving the cabin on Bear Ridge Trail and heading home for the night, Brandon had asked for her phone number. He said he would call on Sunday afternoon. In between a trip to Lakewood Galleria Mall with her mom and working on her required summer reading of *Lord of the Flies*, it was all Jonie could think about.

She was jolted from her thoughts by the sound she'd been waiting for. She tossed *Lord of the Flies* on her pillow without putting her bookmark in place. The phone rang three times before it stopped. She held her breath.

"Jonie, it's for you!" her mom yelled. She scrambled off her bed and raced downstairs. A few steps from the kitchen, she stopped and walked, trying to catch her breath.

She took the beige phone receiver from her mother's outstretched hand and walked down the hall, the spiral phone cord stretching tight, before she put it to her ear.

"Hello?"

"Is this Jonie?" Brandon said hesitantly.

Jonie started laughing.

"Uhm, yes! Who else would it be?"

"Gosh, I don't know." Brandon chuckled. Then they were quiet. Jonie had never talked to a boy she liked on the phone. She wondered if this was Brandon's first time talking to a girl on the phone. *No way,* she thought, just as quickly as the thought entered her mind. *He probably had a line of girls calling him every night.*

"How was church?" Jonie finally asked.

"Boring, as usual."

Jonie looked around for somewhere to sit. She could go back into the kitchen and sit at the table, but then her mother could hear her. She sighed and sat down in the carpeted hallway, leaning against the wall and stretching her legs as far out in front of her as they'd go.

"Are you still there?" Brandon asked. "Hello?"

"Oh, sorry!" Jonie's face turned crimson. "Just got a little distracted. What are you doing the rest of the day?"

"Maybe watch baseball with my dad. The Yankees are on. I thought about going to the park to hang with some buddies and swim. It's so hot today."

Jonie had never been to the pool on one of her days off. Suddenly, a thought occurred to her: was Brandon about to ask her to go to the pool today? Would that be a date? Her mind started a frenzy of questions. Jonie waited for him to continue, but there was just awkward silence.

"Okay, well, I guess I'll get off here," he said after what felt like ten minutes. "I'm going to call Kyle and see if he wants to swim."

Nope, not a date, Jonie thought, a feeling of disappointment rushing over her.

"Oh, okay," she replied hesitantly. "Have fun at the pool..."

"Bye, Jonie." The sound of the dial tone filled her right ear. She looked at her watch: almost three in the afternoon. Outside, the sun was shining, and the skies were clear. She jumped up and sprinted toward the kitchen, slamming the phone receiver back in its place.

"Mom!"

"What, dear?" Nancy was sitting at the mahogany dining room table with the Sunday newspaper spread all around.

"What are you up to?"

"I'm looking for a used piano. I was thinking about giving lessons again."

"That sounds like a good idea." Jonie was half paying attention. "Hey, it's a pretty day outside—let's go to the pool! I can bring you for free."

Nancy put down the classified section and picked up her mug of coffee. As she sipped, she looked out the window over the kitchen sink.

"That sounds like a great idea," she finally said. "Just us gals."

"Okay, I'm going to change," Jonie said. "I can be ready in ten minutes."

"That soon?"

"Yep." Jonie gently pulled her mom's hand until she was standing. "We want to grab chairs and an umbrella, if there are any left, and have the entire afternoon to relax!"

"Okay, you're right." Her mom started to tidy up her pile of newspaper clippings.

"We don't have time for that, Mom!" Jonie yelled over her shoulder as she ran back up to her bedroom. She opened the bottom drawer of her dresser and found the one swimsuit she had. Jonie didn't own a dozen swimsuits like other girls her age did.

Twenty-five minutes later, Jonie and her mother pulled into the park pool's gravel lot.

"Gosh, this place is packed!" Nancy said as they drove around twice in search of an empty space. Finally, she zipped into one, and the two of them hopped out of the car and made a beeline to the front entrance.

"Jonie!" Jennifer greeted from behind the counter at the check-in window. "You're here on your day off!"

"I sure am! I just couldn't pass up this nice afternoon."

"Have fun. Nice to see you, Mrs. K."

As Nancy smiled and pushed through the turnstile, Jonie lingered. She leaned in toward the counter and whispered to Jennifer.

"Have you seen Brandon?"

"He's off today, I think."

"He is, but he might be here with Kyle."

"Oh, gotcha. He hasn't come through yet, but if he does, I'll get on the intercom and let you know."

"Don't you dare!" Jonie laughed, and her face turned red, even though she knew her friend was joking. Or at least she hoped so.

Jennifer pointed toward a group of people gathered in front of the window.

"Keep moving, love bird, you're holding up my line."

Jonie jogged to catch up to her mom, who was waiting underneath a maple tree.

"Gosh, I haven't been swimming in years. Is that the concession stand?" Nancy said as they walked toward the glistening swimming pool. Jonie glanced over at her mom, who seemed like she was all over the place.

"I bet you'll see someone you..." Jonie began. Before she could finish her sentence, her mom's voice rang out.

"Hey Theresa! So good to see you!" Nancy shifted her duffel bag to her other shoulder and gave her friend a hug. She gestured and laughed as if she came to the pool every day.

Standing off to the side, Jonie eagerly scanned the crowd.

"Mom, I'm going to go find some chairs," she said after a few minutes. She wasn't sure if her mother heard her, but she wandered off anyway.

After a few minutes, she still hadn't spotted Brandon. And she figured if he saw her, he would come over and say hello. But doubt crept into her mind as she finally found two empty lounge chairs. She set her bag on one and placed her beach towel on the other to reserve it for her mom. She rubbed sunscreen on her face and shoulders, and then she laid back in the chair.

After what felt like twenty minutes, Jonie sensed someone near her, and she jerked her eyes open with nervous anticipation.

It was just her mother.

"It took me forever to find you!" Nancy shaded her eyes from the sun and looked down at her daughter.

"Sorry, Mom, I must have dozed off. I saved you a seat." Jonie patted the chair next to her, and Nancy stretched out on it.

"Do you think I'll get to meet your boss?"

Jonie wondered when her mother would ask. And for a split second before they'd left the house, Jonie had considered not coming to the pool with her mom for that very reason. But then the idea of seeing Brandon outside of work was too enticing.

"I don't know," Jonie said, which wasn't a lie. "I don't know if she works on Sundays." That was a total lie. Ms. Livingston worked every day the pool was open.

Hmm, she suddenly wondered. *What does Ms. Livingston do when the pool isn't open?* Which was, she counted to herself, about seven months out of the year. The question intrigued her.

"Mom, let's just relax and have some fun." Jonie stretched out a little more on the lounge chair.

"I'm going to take a dip in the pool. Want me to teach you how to swim today?"

Jonie slid her sunglasses down her nose and stared at her mother.

"No, thank you."

"Suit yourself."

Jonie sighed and looked around. Where was Brandon? Maybe she hadn't heard right and he wasn't coming at all. She wasn't listening that well, anyway, she knew, which was why Brandon seemed to get off the phone so quickly. She carefully eyed the perimeter of the pool but didn't see any groups of guys hanging out. It was mostly families.

And then there was her mother, who had taught herself to doggy paddle as a kid but didn't learn beyond that. Jonie watched in half amusement and half mortification as her mother, with cheap goggles fastened tightly to her head, slowly doggy paddled the length of the pool. She tried her best to stay within the lines that marked a swimming lane, but Jonie could tell her goggles were fogging up and making that impossible.

Jonie sighed again. Maybe Brandon would show up later. Or maybe he wouldn't. She would be lying to herself if she said she wasn't disappointed.

Or maybe, she thought, *he regretted mentioning it and decided not to come because she might show up.*

As she considered this, her face turned red with irritation. *Does he not want to hang out with me?* She thought. *Was it because somehow he knows I don't have twenty-six adorable two-piece swimsuits to choose from?*

"Jonie!"

Jolted out of her racing thoughts, she looked up to see her mother walking toward her, dripping a trail of water.

"Your face is looking a little pink," Nancy said as she dried her hair then wiped smudged mascara from under her eyes. "Did you not put sunscreen on?"

"Maybe I need some more," Jonie mumbled. And while she knew that she didn't actually need sunscreen, she fished it out of her bag and put some on anyway.

"You missed a spot," Nancy said as she opened a book.

"You're not even looking!" Jonie laughed, and she squirted some sunscreen on the palm of her hand and rubbed it all over her mom's arm.

"Hey!" Nancy put down the book on the small plastic table between them and rubbed the sunscreen in until it disappeared.

"Which book is that?" Jonie moved her sunglasses down her nose and peered over them at the Mary Higgins Clark paperback laying on the table. She picked it up. "Oh yeah! *Moonlight Becomes You.* That's a good one."

"Wait." Nancy grabbed the book out of Jonie's reach. "You're too young to be reading this."

"It's a little late for that, Mom. I've been stealing your copies for years."

"Oh, Lord. I won't even ask what else you've been doing." Jonie knew her mom was joking. Unfortunately, Jonie didn't really have anything more exciting than that to tell her mother.

But maybe, just maybe, that would all change if she could get to know Brandon more.

She looked around the pool one more time. She felt silly and irritated.

"You know it's the funeral director, right?" Jonie said to her mom.

"What?!" Nancy's jaw dropped. "Why did you just ruin the ending for me?"

"I don't know," Jonie groaned. But she knew why. She was irritated that her grand afternoon plans weren't working out. It had felt like a good idea to be sassy toward her mother, but then she felt bad, as she normally did, and suddenly, she just wanted to go home.

"I'm sorry. I don't know why I said that."

"I do," Nancy replied. "Because you're a teenager. And that means you're crazy."

"Yeah, you're probably right," Jonie laughed. "Hey, let's go home. I think I am burning."

"Okay. I'm kind of hungry, anyway, and those hotdogs at the concession stand do not look very good, sorry to tell you."

"Uhm, no, the first rule of the park pool is to never eat the hotdogs." Jonie slipped her feet into flip flops, pushed her sunglasses up on her head, and followed her mother, who was already heading toward the women's locker room.

As she walked, she kept her head down, not daring to look around the pool again. She felt embarrassed that she'd jumped so quickly to see Brandon when she didn't even know for sure if he'd be there. It wasn't like she didn't have plenty of things to do at home.

A few moments later, just as she was about to walk through the turnstile door to exit the pool, she heard someone say her name.

It was Ms. Livingston.

"Hi!" Jonie said, turning around. "How's it going today?"

"It's the usual. I haven't seen you here before on one of your days off."

"Yeah, it's weird. I keep expecting someone to come up to me and ask for help doing something."

Ms. Livingston smiled, and then looked at Jonie's mother standing next to her.

"Oh, right!" Jonie said. "This is my mom, Nancy."

Ms. Livingston reached out her hand. "I'm Alice. It's nice to meet you. Your daughter is a great employee. She's one of the hardest working staff members I have."

Jonie smiled inside. Ms. Livingston *did* like her. One day Jonie thought she did, the next day she just wasn't sure. But Ms. Livingston would never lie to someone's mom. No way.

"Well, thank you, that's good to hear," Nancy said, beaming. "This is a great place, how long have you worked here?"

"Well, let's see." Ms. Livingston paused. "My parents opened it in the nineteen sixties when I was a teenager, and I started working here that very summer. And it's nineteen ninety-nine, so I've been working here for thirty-four years."

Jonie noticed a strange look pass over her face after she finished doing that bit of math in her head.

"That's great, just great," Nancy said. "Jonie sure likes it here. She talks about it all the time. We're thankful that you gave her this job."

"Jonie will always have a place here at the pool if she wants it."

Wow! Jonie thought. She tried to hide her excitement; she could work at the park pool every summer for the rest of high school and maybe even during college.

"Thanks, Ms. Livingston." Jonie hoped her voice actually wasn't as high-pitched as it sounded in her own ears. "I really appreciate that."

Nancy moved her duffel bag to her other shoulder.

"So, Alice," she began. "Is it just you here, or..."

Before her mother had a chance to finish the question, Jonie gently grabbed her hand.

"Mom, I really need to get home! My back, uhm, feels really sunburned, and I should put some aloe lotion on it." And she tugged at her mom's arm, leading her toward the exit.

Looking confused, Nancy waved at Ms. Livingston, and Jonie breathed a sigh of relief.

~

Alice watched Jonie and her mother leave through the front gate, their laughter trailing behind them. Out of habit, she walked into the women's locker room for a cleanliness check, her sandals echoing softly against the damp tile.

She checked each stall, fixed the stuck paper towel dispenser, and picked up an empty soda can off the floor. At the sink, she turned on the water and washed her hands, watching the suds spiral down the drain.

Thirty-four years, she thought, catching her reflection in the mirror. Her hazel eyes were steady but a little tired. Gentle wrinkles fanned from their corners. She smiled at herself, a big one that deepened the wrinkles, and she shut off the tap.

Five o'clock was creeping close. Alice enjoyed Sundays when she could leave work and still have an entire evening free. And this evening, she had plans.

An hour later, as the last family waved goodbye and walked toward their car, she locked up her office, left the paperwork on her desk for tomorrow, and stepped out into the evening.

People always assumed managing a public place like a swimming pool meant you loved being around people all the time. But what Alice looked forward to most were quiet evenings, when the noise and the water and the constant motion all finally settled.

Tonight, she had plans to go see a movie and enjoy a bucket of popcorn for dinner.

As she walked toward her cabin, she caught herself thinking about how nice it would be to have someone to call. Someone who'd meet her at the theater and then linger afterward to talk about it all: the actors, the good parts, the dumb parts, the music. At the theater, she always saw them: couples, families, groups of teenagers clustered under the marquee lights, laughing and comparing favorite scenes. And sometimes, but not always, she wished she could join them.

Fifteen years ago, Alice did have that. She and Keith had done everything together. The only time they weren't side by side was when Alice was at the pool. Even then, Keith would pop in occasionally to say hi while he was out and about in town or on his way home from work.

They had been inseparable. When the pool closed down after each summer, he and Alice went on adventures all the time. Their favorite was long, early-morning hikes through the forests of Twin Pines followed by a big breakfast at a nearby buffet restaurant. Autumn was actually Alice's favorite season, when the gentle hills of the Enchanted Mountains were peppered with every shade of red, orange, and green imaginable.

Even though they lived at Twin Pines, the park was big enough to still be their getaway. She and Keith would sometimes stay in a different cabin on the weekends, a secluded one at the end of Horseshoe Trail that didn't have electricity. They'd build a fire early in the morning to make their coffee and end their day with another fire to stay warm before crawling under layers of down blankets and flannel sheets.

At nearly six o'clock, Alice locked her front door and threw her sweater and purse into the passenger's seat of her white Plymouth Neon. The evening light spilled across the windshield, and she felt the tightness in her chest begin to ease.

She still had plenty of time before the show started. Enough to get her ticket, popcorn, and her favorite seat: right in the middle of the top row. From that seat, she felt like the whole theater belonged to her.

And for a little while, in the dark, with the glow of the screen washing over her, Alice could pretend the only care she had in the world was finishing that huge bucket of popcorn.

Chapter 6

Later that week, Alice stood on the top step of the gazebo, finishing the morning huddle, when she spotted a short, heavy-set man in a suit wandering near the pool entrance. His left arm rested behind him, his right hand held a plaid driver hat to his chest, and he peered around as if inspecting every inch of his surroundings.

Even from that distance, Alice knew the stance, the hat, the way he bent at the waist as he looked at things: Jerry London. She grimaced, feeling that familiar flicker of nerves. He never changed. Grocery store, bank, gas station; no matter where he was, Jerry always looked like he'd stepped straight out of another decade.

Alice quickly finished the huddle and walked toward the pool entrance.

"Good morning, there, Alice," Jerry called, shielding his eyes as he glanced up at the pale blue sky. "Nice day to have a swimming pool."

Nice day to have a swimming pool. His line never changed. If it rained, he'd say, "Rough day to have a swimming pool." If he ever greeted her differently, she'd assume he'd finally lost his mind.

"What can I do for you, Jerry? We're opening soon, and there's a lot to do."

Jerry checked his watch, the band nearly lost in his thick arm hair. "It's not even nine. We can talk for a few minutes, can't we?"

"Of course," Alice said, though she didn't mean it. The last time he'd been in her office, a "few minutes" had turned into nearly an hour. "Why don't you walk with me to the concession stand? I could use some help unpacking boxes."

Without waiting for an answer, she turned and headed toward the other side of the pool. Jerry arrived at the concession stand behind her, slightly out of breath and already sweating through his shirt.

"I'll show up at city hall looking like I've worked a full day on a farm," he huffed and puffed.

Alice cracked a thin smile. "Don't you have a council meeting or grand opening somewhere this morning?"

"Later. Ribbon-cutting ceremony for that new senior center. I helped to secure funding for it."

"Hand me those scissors," Alice said. She quickly opened a box of plastic drink lids, hundreds of them crammed inside.

"Jackpot!" Jerry grinned. "You're set for years."

For a few moments, Alice quietly put away the supplies before finally breaking the silence.

"Jerry, what exactly are you doing here?"

"Well now, I don't want to be a bother. But—if I am, you just say so. I know you don't think retirement's an option, just like your parents. It's hard to find that kind of work ethic anymore."

Alice kept unpacking boxes, trying to ignore the sound of his voice and the way he leaned against the counter watching her. When she opened one cupboard and found it already full of lids, she muttered, "Guess I didn't need to order these after all."

Jerry chuckled, but Alice turned to face him. "Jerry, I really have to get to work."

He lifted his hands in mock surrender. "Of course, of course. Just... keep me in mind, should you ever decide to sell. I could have you on a beach somewhere inside of a week."

There it is, she thought. *Took him long enough*. She watched him walk away toward the parking lot, his hat tucked under his arm.

~

Jerry London hated to sweat. Yet every time he saw Alice Livingston, he couldn't stop.

He'd been sweating around her since high school, sitting behind her in alphabetical order, staring at the back of her head. Alice was quiet, smart, and impossible to read.

Now, sliding into his baby-blue Crown Victoria, Jerry cranked the air conditioning to full blast. As he turned out of the gravel lot, the car's undercarriage scraped harshly.

"Good grief. First thing I'll do when I own this place is pave the dang parking lot."

His father had spent years trying to buy the pool from Alice's dad. Jerry still remembered tagging along one afternoon on a visit to the Livingstons' cabin. He'd been sixteen, and it was the first time he had been around Alice outside of school. When Mrs. Livingston opened the door and Alice was standing there, Jerry had nearly forgotten how to speak.

Alice's dark blonde hair hung in loose curls on her shoulders, and her wide-set hazel eyes seemed to size Jerry up. He was intimidated and fascinated. Alice had looked right at him...and then past him. The moment lasted seconds, but it stuck with Jerry for decades.

His father and the Livingstons talked business at the kitchen table, and Jerry sat there sweating through his heavy cotton polo shirt, half listening, half wondering what Alice was doing upstairs. Jerry left that house knowing two things: he'd never been more embarrassed in his life as he tried to hide the sweat stains under his arms, and he'd somehow fallen for a girl who barely knew he existed.

Decades later, he'd built a good life: law school, his own practice, a seat on city council. But the dream of the pool lingered. Maybe it was nostalgia, maybe it was unfinished family business. Or maybe it was just Alice.

He didn't kid himself anymore about winning her heart, even though she still made him as nervous as he felt that first time seeing her at her family's cabin. But owning the pool? That still felt like something he was meant to do. All he needed was to make Alice an offer she couldn't refuse.

As he pulled into the parking lot of the new senior center, preparing for the ribbon-cutting, Jerry straightened his tie and imagined the next one he'd host: standing in front of Alice's pool, scissors in hand, claiming the dream that had haunted him for decades.

~

"So, Jonie Baloney, what'd you do for the Fourth of July?" Brandon asked.

"Worked. You?"

"Same." He grinned. "You saw me showing off my lifeguard skills."

"Skills? On a scale of one to ten—"

As Jonie spoke, Brandon waved both hands in front of her face, wiggling his fingers dramatically.

"—I'd give it that," Jonie said, pushing one hand down.

"Harsh! You're breaking my heart."

Rain pattered on the gazebo roof. The pool had just cleared; parents gathered their belongings, and teenagers huddled by the concession stand with wet towels wrapped around their shoulders.

"Did you see Ms. L talking to that guy the other day? Think it's her boyfriend?"

Jonie laughed. "Her boyfriend? Please. He looked like he was twice her age and dressed in some costume from the seventeen hundreds."

"Still, he was helping her unload boxes. Gentlemanly, if you ask me."

"He *did* look familiar," Jonie said thoughtfully. "I've seen him in the newspaper or something."

"Mayor?"

"Nope. The mayor's a woman."

"Oh, yeah." Brandon scratched his head, his messy black hair sticking up. It looked like he hadn't had a haircut all summer. Jonie caught herself staring and looked away quickly.

"I think we should go on a date," Brandon said out of nowhere.

Jonie's heart jumped. *Finally.*

"Sure," she said, realizing immediately that she sounded too casual in her effort to be cool. She quickly added, "That sounds great!"

"How about a movie Friday night? *Austin Powers*?"

"Perfect." Then Jonie remembered that she'd have to tell her parents, and she immediately started feeling nervous. Her dad always joked that she couldn't date until she was forty years old. She knew things could get awkward.

"There's just one thing..." Jonie said, as she played with the drawstring on her shorts. "Well, you see, I've never, well, not really...so I may need to..."

"You need to ask your parents' permission?" Brandon asked casually, as if it was the most normal thing in the world. Jonie felt instantly relieved that he didn't think it was a big deal.

"Probably so, I think." Jonie tried to be nonchalant. "You?"

"Yeah. Sorta. I mean, I just let them know what I'm up to."

They grinned at each other. Brandon glanced toward the sky. "It looks like the rain is clearing up, we'll have to get back at it soon. Are you hungry?"

"Maybe. What are the specials?"

He squinted toward the concession stand. "Lobster with champagne. Or steak with shrimp."

"I'll take the lobster, and you can have my champagne."

"Coming right up!" Jonie laughed as Brandon sprinted toward the stand and ordered two bags of Cheetos and two cans of Orange Crush.

Chapter 7

Alice prided herself on keeping things steady: her pool, her staff, her schedule, her life. If something went wrong, she handled it with the same firm efficiency she applied to everything else.

Which meant she hated surprises.

And Jerry showing up at her pool at eight-thirty on a Tuesday morning, wearing that smug half-smile and talking about buying the pool, *again*, was precisely the kind of surprise she couldn't stand.

He always came unannounced. Four times a year, at least. Always "just stopping by." It was clear that he hadn't outgrown being the same annoying kid who pulled her ponytail, hid her notebook, and took forever to get the hint after she said no to being his date for the junior *and* senior prom.

Same with the pool. She'd told him she wasn't interested in selling it more times than she could count. Her parents had told his father no, too, twenty years earlier. The Londons, it seemed, had an inherited allergy to that particular word.

Alice could still picture the first time Mr. London came to their house: her mother offered him coffee in their sunny kitchen, and her father kept his tone polite but firm. Jerry had been there, sitting beside his father in a crisp, ironed polo. She'd been bored out of her mind and escaped upstairs with the excuse of homework.

She smiled faintly at the memory, remembering that Jerry had actually looked cute trying to look polite in front of her parents. This was before Alice got to know who Jerry really was: annoyingly persistent and full of himself.

She felt her face grow hot with irritation. She also was fairly certain that several of her employees had seen Jerry talking to her at the concession stand. The last thing she needed was for her teenage staff to start whispering.

She knew that people in town already talked enough. About her past and how she mostly kept to herself. She had no desire to give them more material.

Back in her office, she sat at her desk, tapping a pen against a stack of forms. Then, with an abrupt scrape of her chair, she stood. The back of it clanged against the metal shelf behind her.

"That's it. This ends today."

Alice yanked open the bottom drawer of her desk, pulled out a thick telephone book, its cover curling at the edges, and flipped to City Government.

"Councilman Jerry London," she mumbled as her finger ran down the list of names. Finally, she found it.

The phone rang. Once. Twice. Four times. Just as Alice was about to hang up, his answering machine clicked on.

"Hello, this is Jerry London, your city councilman. I deeply apologize for not being able to answer your important call right now. I'm probably somewhere in our beautiful city trying to make it better for you."

Alice rolled her eyes like she saw her teenage staff members do all the time.

"Please leave your message, and my secretary will get back to you as soon as possible. Thanks again!"

Finally, the beep.

"Jerry, this is Alice Livingston at the Twin Pines State Park swimming pool." Her tone was crisp and efficient. "Please call me back at your earliest convenience with a time I can come by your office to discuss something important."

She hung up, feeling good. The thought of marching into his fancy downtown office, looking him straight in the eye, and telling him, once and for all, that he was not welcome at her pool unless he paid admission like everyone else made her smile.

And then, to her own surprise, she laughed: a short, bright laugh that filled her office and startled her with how long it had been since she'd heard it.

~

Jonie was both impatient and terrified to get home that evening. She needed to ask her parents' permission to go on a date with Brandon, a boy they'd never met or even heard of, and she wanted the whole ordeal to be over with as soon as possible.

When she got home, she rushed upstairs to change out of her work clothes and take a quick shower before dinner. Standing in her bedroom with the door closed halfway, she heard her father yell up the stairs.

"What toppings do you want on your pizza?"

She stopped towel drying her hair and thought for a moment.

"I'll eat whatever you guys get!" she yelled back. She figured she'd be as accommodating as possible. Maybe it would increase her chances of them allowing her to go out with Brandon.

She threw on her comfy clothes and walked downstairs, where her dad was watching the evening news and her mother was reaching into a kitchen cabinet for plates.

"Hey, wonderful parents of mine!" Jonie strolled into the living room and flopped down on the couch. Both of her parents looked at her in surprise. Then Jonie saw them look at each other and raise their eyebrows slightly.

Maybe I need to dial it down a little, Jonie thought.

"How was work?" Nancy asked. She walked into the living room and sat down on the couch beside her husband.

"Fine!" Jonie and her dad said at the same time.

"You go first," Jonie laughed.

"Oh no, by all means..." Allen gestured and turned his attention back to the news.

"It was busy, as usual," Jonie said to her mother. "I drank, like, ten gallons of water because I was sweating so much."

"Have you learned to swim yet?" Allen asked, popping a pretzel into his mouth and not looking away from the television.

"No, Dad." *Actually*, Jonie thought to herself. *Why haven't I? Maybe Brandon could teach me.* The idea of it made her smile.

She brought her focus back to the living room and her parents.

"Actually, speaking of work, there's this person there who asked me..."

Suddenly, the doorbell rang.

"All right, dinner is here!" Allen clapped his hands as he jumped up from the couch and reached into his back pocket for his wallet. Feeling annoyed at the interruption, Jonie took the opportunity to get her thoughts together before she tried broaching the subject again.

A minute later, Allen closed the front door and brought the pizzas into the kitchen. Jonie and her mother followed behind, each grabbing a plate and a napkin. Back in the living room, Jonie let her parents take a few bites of pizza before she tried making her announcement again.

"Like I was saying." Jonie swallowed a mouthful of pizza toppings. "There's this friend I made at work, and we'd like to go to the movies this Friday. There's a new movie coming out that's supposed to be, like, the funniest movie. I think it starts around eight. I should be back home by ten thirty."

Once Jonie started talking, she couldn't stop, and she could tell that her parents were overloaded with information.

"This Friday?" her dad said with a mouthful of food. "A movie? I haven't been to a movie in forever."

"Oh! Oh, well, I didn't mean..." Then she saw her mom wink at her.

"Ha, ha, very funny," Jonie threw a couch pillow at her dad.

"Hey!" Allen said as it barely missed knocking his plate full of pizza crusts onto his lap.

"Who is this friend?" Nancy asked. "Is it Jennifer?"

"Uh, no," Jonie said as she felt her face turn pink. "Remember that day we went to the pool a few weeks ago? My friend was supposed to be there but ended up not coming. I was going to introduce you."

"What's her name?" Allen said. "Maybe I've met her dad."

"His name is Brandon Murphy."

Nancy looked at her husband. Then she looked at Jonie with a strange little smile on her face.

"Jonie has a boyfriend!" she said with a laugh. Allen, who didn't exactly have a smile on his face, looked at his wife and shook his head. She playfully hit him on the arm.

However Jonie had expected her parents to react, this was not it.

"Uhm, he isn't my boyfriend," Jonie stammered. As soon as she said the word "boyfriend," her face turned a crimson red.

"He *is* her boyfriend!" Nancy said.

"No he isn't!" Jonie's face turned an impossibly deeper shade of crimson. Allen smiled at his daughter as he stood up from the couch and walked into the kitchen. He returned with another slice of pizza. As he reached the couch, he paused, and then went back into the kitchen and put another slice of pizza on his plate.

"What movie did you say you were going to see?" he asked as he sat back down.

Jonie breathed a sigh of relief. Her parents hadn't actually said, "Yes, you can go to the movies with this strange boy we've never met," but she knew she was in the clear. She felt more relaxed than she had all night, and her appetite returned. She jumped up from the couch and went into the kitchen for more pizza.

"We haven't totally decided yet. But *Austin Powers* is supposed to be super funny."

"I've heard it's a good movie. We might have to go see it with you all." Allen smiled.

"No! I would just absolutely die."

Jonie knew that her mother would want to hear more about Brandon. And Jonie didn't mind. In fact, she was looking forward to it. Besides Jennifer, she hadn't been able to talk to anyone about him, except for that one awkward time with Mrs. Livingston. But that totally didn't count.

By the time Jonie finished her pizza, her parents were engrossed in *Wheel of Fortune.* Her father was working hard to try to solve the puzzle in his favorite category of "food & drink."

After absentmindedly watching for a while, the day caught up with Jonie, and she suddenly felt tired. But she had one thing left to do. She told her parents goodnight and grabbed the phone receiver from off the kitchen wall. She pulled the cord around the corner and down the hallway as far as she could. She didn't want to wait until tomorrow: she wanted to call Brandon and tell him that she officially could go to the movies with him on Friday.

The phone rang four times before Brandon picked up. Jonie, as always, thought about how lucky he was that he got his own private line. What she wouldn't give for her own phone and her own line. Now that she was dating, maybe her parents would see how sophisticated and grownup she was and let her have one. Especially, she thought, if she offered to pay for it out of the money she was earning at the park pool.

"Hey Jonie!"

"Hey," she said, startled. "How did you know it was me?"

"Your number showed up on the caller ID."

"I forget about that."

"Yeah, it's that new-fangled technology that everyone is talking about."

"Shut up," Jonie said as she scratched a bug bite on her left calf. "I just wanted to tell you that my parents said it was cool for me to go to the movies with you on Friday."

"Oh, good." He sounded distracted, and suddenly Jonie felt self-conscious. She thought that Brandon sounded like he didn't really care.

"Did you ask *your* parents?"

"Nah, I don't really need to. I have my own car, I just have to be back by curfew and they're happy."

Jonie felt so embarrassed. She felt like a little girl, and she wished she'd never told Brandon about having to ask for her parents' permission.

"I see," Jonie said. Suddenly, she felt super tired and all she wanted was to crawl into bed.

"Okay, that's all," she said quickly.

"See you tomorrow, Jonie Baloney."

Jonie couldn't help herself. Her face broke out into a huge smile.

"See you tomorrow, Brandon."

~

That evening, Alice sat on her porch with a cup of tea cooling between her palms. The pool lights were off, the crickets were noisy, and the hum of Twin Pines at night filled the silence like a familiar companion: soft chatter from the campground, a car door closing somewhere in the distance.

Throughout the day, she'd thought about calling Jerry again, as she rehearsed in her mind what she'd say to him. She had his home phone number, because he'd given her every possible contact number he had. But she didn't dial it.

Still, her thoughts drifted to him and how he'd looked that morning in that ridiculous hat and too-heavy clothing, pretending he was just casually passing through on his way into town.

Alice set her tea down with a sigh. She wasn't sure what annoyed her more: that Jerry still knew how to get under her skin after all these years, or that a small part of her might miss the challenge once it was gone.

Chapter 8

Jerry looked at his secretary with disdain.

"Tell me again, Melanie," he said, his voice steady and icy. "When did she call and leave this message?"

Melanie shifted in her chair behind her giant desk, cluttered with papers, manila folders, and yellow slips of paper scrawled with notes.

"Well," she said, picking up one of the slips with her long, teal-manicured fingers. "According to this, Alice Livingston called last Monday around ten in the morning."

"According to 'that.'" Jerry nodded his head at the paper in Meredith's hand. "And is that your handwriting?"

Melanie glanced down at the paper. "It is."

Jerry sighed for the tenth time that morning. "This is a very important potential client. I simply don't understand how you forgot to give me this message."

He was already sweating, and he could feel it through his dress shirt. He removed his sport coat and draped it over one arm and began fanning himself with his hat.

"I don't want this to happen again. Consider yourself warned."

Melanie stared at him, her hands flat on the desk like two tan starfish. She said nothing, but her cheeks were flushed. Jerry snatched the yellow slip of paper off her desk and marched into his office, slamming the door.

He sat in his desk chair, swiveling nervously and tapping his pencil on his knee. What *did* Alice want? Had she changed her mind? Was she ready to accept his offer? He couldn't think of any other reason why Alice, who had never called him in her entire life, would be calling now. Finally, Jerry thought, his lawyerly skills of persuasion had paid off.

Jerry studied the slip. Melanie had written down Alice's number, though he didn't need it. He had it memorized since that day he visited her cabin with his dad. It hadn't changed after all these years.

Pushing back his chair, Jerry picked up the telephone receiver and dialed. It rang twice.

"Twin Pines State Park Swimming Pool," a young woman's voice rang out cheerfully. "Jonie speaking, how may I help you today?"

"May I speak to Alice Livingston, please? This is Councilman Jerry London." His voice was full of business urgency. "It's important."

"One moment, please." Jerry's ear was filled with the sound of light classical music. Suddenly, the music stopped.

"This is Alice Livingston."

Jerry wasn't expecting her to answer so quickly. He cleared his throat before speaking.

"Alice, this is Jerry."

Silence.

"Jerry London," he said awkwardly. "I'm returning your call. You, uh, called me."

"I did. At least a week ago."

Jerry sensed the familiar edge in her voice, even more pointed than usual. He cringed.

"Well, yes, this is true. There was a misunderstanding with my secretary, but it won't happen again. I apologize for my tardiness."

Silence filled the other side of the call.

"So," he continued, beads of sweat beginning to roll down his forehead. "What can I do for you?"

"I'd like to talk about something important. When would be a good time for me to come by your office?"

"Come by my office?" Jerry could barely get the words out.

"Yes, Jerry."

"Can you hold on a moment?"

Jerry practically ran from his office to the reception area. Melanie was leaning over in her chair, adjusting a shiny gold ring on her second toe.

"Melanie!" he whispered loudly. "Clear my calendar for Monday! I don't want interruptions."

"Okay," she said hesitantly, flipping through the leather-bound calendar book. "Wait. You have a meeting with the deputy mayor first thing Monday morning."

"Cancel it!" Jerry almost shouted.

Melanie looked up at Jerry, her face full of worry. "It took me so long to get that scheduled. Are you sure?"

But Jerry was beyond reasoning with. Alice Livingston had never asked for a meeting. His moment had come. He could feel the sun on his back, and he could smell the chlorine in the air. He returned to his office, picked up the receiver, and pressed the hold button.

"Alice," he said, a little breathless.

"Jerry. I'm still here. What happened?"

"Logistics," he said flippantly. "I'm free all day Monday. Tell me what time works for you."

"Noon. It won't take long."

What won't take long? Jerry wondered, but he didn't dare ask questions.

"Okay, then. Noon Monday it is. I look forward to seeing you, Alice."

He barely slept a wink all weekend.

~

It was finally Friday, the night of Jonie and Brandon's first real date, and Jonie was jittery with excitement. When she caught Ms. Livingston occupied with the landscapers and Brandon focused on telling some kids to stop running, she knew it was the perfect moment to sneak out from work just a few minutes early.

She slipped out through the side gate, past the rows of damp lounge chairs and ducked behind a thick patch of rhododendrons. From there, she could still hear everything: splashing, laughter, and the shrill lifeguard whistle cutting through the sticky late-afternoon air.

The pool was packed again, the way it always was near the end of summer when families tried to squeeze out the last bit of vacation before school started. Beyond the fence, the sun was sinking behind the ridge, streaking the tops of the pine trees gold. The whole park hummed with sounds: crickets tuning up, a radio playing faintly from someone's picnic site, the distant splash of kayak paddles from the lake.

Jonie hugged her arms around herself and waited, heart fluttering, as a car door slammed in the parking lot. It was a family loading up their cooler, the dad whistling off-key as he wrestled to shove it in the trunk.

Finally, she saw her dad steer Buttercup into the gravel parking lot. She hurriedly tossed her bag into the backseat and climbed into the front.

"Hey Dad! Let's go!"

"Gosh, where's the fire?" he asked, glancing at the pool.

"Very funny. I just have a lot to do."

"Ah, yes. Tonight's the big date."

"Yes, Dad." Jonie fastened her seatbelt, feeling impatient.

"Are you going to wear a prom dress?"

"No! Why would I do that?"

"Well, I don't know." Allen smiled. "What time is this young man picking you up?"

"Six forty-five."

"Will you two dine somewhere elegant?"

"Either Art's Diner or the exclusive Movies 10 buffet."

"Popcorn, nachos, Pepsi, and heartburn?"

"That's the one!" Jonie laughed.

As soon as Jonie got home, she tore into the house to get ready. The night that her parents had given her permission to go, before she fell asleep, Jonie had spent almost forty-five minutes rummaging through her closet trying to find the perfect outfit.

Now, as she dried her hair, she could see in the mirror the three outfits she had chosen. Jonie looked at her watch. Brandon would be there in fifteen minutes, and she felt like she still had so much to do.

Finally, she threw on her light-pink sundress and matching cardigan and slipped her tanned feet into the new flip flops she'd bought for this date. Just as she turned off the bedroom light, the front doorbell rang.

Perfect timing, she thought, and a huge grin spread across her face. But just as she thought she would reach the front door before her parents, they both rushed in front of her and grabbed for the door handle. Nancy actually stuck her tongue out at Jonie as she reached the door first.

So much for my mom being the normal one tonight, Jonie thought. When the door swung open, Brandon stood there, smiling and cool as a cucumber.

"Welcome!" Nancy said. "I'm Jonie's mother, Nancy. This is Allen, her father."

Allen held out his hand, and Brandon shook it with a strong grip.

Jonie just wanted to hop into his car and get their date started. But it looked like her parents had other plans.

"Why don't you come in for a minute," Allen said. Brandon looked at Jonie, who then looked at her watch.

"Well, Dad, maybe for just a minute, we have to make sure we aren't late for the movie." Jonie felt her impatience growing already.

"Okay, five minutes, that's all," Allen replied. Jonie sat down on the couch beside Brandon, but not too close.

"So," Nancy said as she crossed her legs and leaned back in the armchair. "How are your parents, Brandon?" She asked the question as if she already knew them.

"They're good, thank you." Brandon was cool and calm, as if he was expecting this entire scene. Jonie figured he'd been through it many times before. Jonie still batted around in her head whether or not she should ask Brandon how many girlfriends he'd had before her. That was, of course, assuming that *she* was his actual girlfriend. They'd never talked about it. But she figured that after their first date tonight, as long as everything went well, she could bring it up.

"What do your parents do?" Nancy continued. Jonie looked down at her watch. Four minutes.

"My father owns the hardware store on Chestnut Street."

"Oh yeah?" Allen interrupted. "I pretty much spend all my free time there."

"And all of our money," Nancy smiled, first at her husband and then at Brandon.

"Hey, that's a good thing for us!" Brandon laughed. Jonie was amazed at how easily he talked to her parents. Was this normal? Jonie's friendships had never been normal. She didn't even remember a time when she'd brought any of her friends over to her house. Jonie had always gone to someone else's, or, more often than that, she simply just didn't have any friends.

"And what does your mother do?" Nancy asked. Suddenly she looked toward the kitchen. "Would you two like something to drink? Maybe a little snack?"

"No, thanks, Mom." Jonie answered quickly before Brandon could, because she knew he would say yes. "We actually need to leave in exactly two minutes."

"To answer your question, Mrs. Kirkland, my mother is a nurse at the hospital across town," Brandon said. "She works night shifts."

"A nurse! Well, if I ever get sick and need to go to the hospital, I'll make sure that I ask for her specifically."

Brandon smiled. Then he looked at Jonie, who did a final check of the time.

"Okay, we have to go," she said, as she stood up and walked toward the door. Brandon stood up as well and shook hands with Allen, and then he reached his arms out and gave Nancy a small hug. Nancy looked over his shoulder at Jonie and gave her a thumbs up. Jonie's face turned bright pink, but she couldn't help smiling.

As the front door closed behind her, Jonie felt the warm evening breeze sweep her hair back, and she breathed a sigh of relief. Finally, the date could begin. She followed Brandon, and he held open the passenger's side door of his dark green Ford Ranger pickup.

As Jonie reached her right hand up to grab her seatbelt, she watched Brandon walk to the driver's side. She'd never seen his hair combed before; it was always a tousled mess at the pool. It looked nice.

Brandon slid into the driver's seat and buckled up. As soon as he started the engine, country music blasted out of the car's speakers.

"Whoa!" Jonie said, as she covered her ears with her hands dramatically.

"Sorry about that, Jonie Baloney. You don't really need those ears anyway."

A few minutes later, Brandon turned down Chestnut Street.

"I'm starving," he said. "How about some Art's? We have time. The stars are out, the moon is full, and I got a pretty lady next to me."

Jonie wanted to roll her eyes at how corny Brandon sounded, but his silliness made her feel happy. She glanced up toward the sky outside her window.

"Sure. But the moon isn't full at all. And it's so cloudy I can't even see it or the stars."

Brandon laughed as he pulled into Art's Drive-In Diner.

"Wow, they're packed!" Brandon said as he circled the parking lot before finally squeezing into a spot. Kids in baseball uniforms raced around with milkshakes and onion rings.

They joined the line, Brandon leaning against the concrete wall of the building with his arm loosely around Jonie's shoulders until it was time to order. They were back at Brandon's truck fifteen minutes later, both carrying brown cardboard boxes filled with footlong hot dogs, onion rings, and sodas.

"I haven't eaten here much," Jonie said with a mouthful of onion rings.

"What? I can't understand you with food in your mouth. So rude." Brandon stuffed two onion rings in his mouth, and Jonie almost choked trying to stifle her laughter.

"My mom doesn't like this place," Jonie was finally able to say. "We rarely get to come. She says it's too greasy"

"That's part of its charm!" Brandon exclaimed.

Moments later, when Jonie reached for the last onion ring, Brandon snatched it instead. As he put it into his mouth, he missed and got ketchup all over his chin. Jonie laughed so hard she almost fell off the hood of his truck.

Twenty minutes later, Brandon pulled into the parking lot of the movie theater. As they walked toward the front doors, Brandon jogged a few steps ahead and reached for the handle.

"Why thank you." Jonie suddenly felt shy.

"Anytime." Brandon smiled as they approached the ticket counter.

"Two for *Austin Powers*, please," Brandon told the man standing behind the counter.

"Now," Brandon said as they took their place in the concessions line. "This is really the most important part of the whole date."

"Oh, is it?" Jonie said, looking up at the menu. "Didn't we just eat enough food for a football team?"

"Nonsense. As I was saying, if you make the mistake of choosing the wrong snack, it will haunt you for the entire movie. Even if it's the best movie in the world, you won't remember that. All you'll remember is that this was the date you went on where the snacks were so terrible you couldn't enjoy yourself."

"Wow," Jonie said, her eyes growing wide. "I didn't realize this was so important. We had better stop talking and focus. I don't want you telling everyone at work that you went on a terrible date with me."

"What can I get you?" the girl behind the counter said. She wore sparkly blue eye shadow, and Jonie thought she recognized her from school.

"Ladies first," Brandon said.

"I'll just take a small Sprite." Jonie reached into her pocket to pull out the twenty-dollar bill her mom had given her before she left the house.

"Your money is no good here," Brandon said. "I'll have a medium popcorn with extra butter and salt and a small Diet Coke."

"Diet Coke?" Jonie asked, trying not to laugh.

"Yeah." Brandon's mouth turned down in a small frown. "I have to watch my figure. I am a lifeguard, you know. My job is to look good while protecting all of those people."

"Ohhh, I see." Jonie laughed.

"Hey, I'm going to go to the gentleman's room before the movie starts. I'll be right back."

"Sure thing." As soon as he disappeared around the corner, Jonie sneaked a handful of Brandon's extra buttery popcorn, even though she was still stuffed from their dinner at Art's.

"Jonie, is that you?" On hearing her name, she turned around and looked right into the smiling face of Ms. Livingston.

"Hi!" Jonie said before remembering that her mouth was full of popcorn, and a piece flew out. Jonie watched in horror as it hit the front of Ms. Livingston's t-shirt and then bounced onto the floor.

Jonie covered her mouth, trying not to laugh and make the situation worse.

"Well, it's good to see you, too," Ms. Livingston smiled as she looked down at her shirt. "I already ate my popcorn, or else I'd throw some at you, as well."

This time, Jonie couldn't contain her laugh.

"I'm so sorry!" She carefully swallowed the rest of her popcorn. "I put way too much in my mouth."

"Yes, I can see that," Ms. Livingston laughed. "Are you enjoying the evening?"

Jonie thought that was a very adult question. She quickly tried to figure out an equally adult response.

"I *am* enjoying this evening, very much so," Jonie said, somewhat slowly, as if she was trying out the combination of words for the first time. "And you?"

"Yes, I am." Ms. Livingston's face looked different to Jonie; younger, maybe. For Jonie, it felt like when she was in elementary school and saw her teacher at the grocery store, and it was so weird because teachers weren't supposed to be anywhere except behind their desk or at the chalkboard.

Suddenly, Brandon reappeared. "Hi, Ms. Livingston," he said, and then he looked over at his popcorn, presumably, Jonie thought, to make sure it was still there.

"Hello, Brandon." Ms. Livingston looked from him to Jonie. "Are you two here together?"

"Yes, ma'am. We are." His eyes beamed, and Jonie's face turned pink and she smiled.

"Are you here to see a movie?" Jonie asked and immediately felt stupid. Why else would someone be at the movie theater?

"Did you see *Austin Powers*?" Brandon asked, with surprise in his voice. Jonie knew that if Ms. Livingston had come to the movies to see *Austin Powers* on a Friday night, she'd totally score extra points with him.

"No, I'm not familiar with that film," Ms. Livingston said. "I saw *The Sixth Sense*. It was about a young boy who sees strange things and the psychiatrist trying to help him. It was fascinating. In fact, it's one of those you'll want to watch twice."

Jonie tried to check the time without turning the soda she was holding upside down.

"We better head on in," Jonie said. "It was good to see you."

"You, as well. Enjoy your movie."

"Thanks!" Jonie and Brandon both said at the same time.

As Jonie gathered her things and began to follow Brandon, Ms. Livingston spoke once again.

"Just a little word of advice."

Jonie's stomach suddenly clenched, and she wondered if this was about Brandon. Whatever Ms. Livingston was going to say about him, she hoped he didn't overhear.

"The best seat in the whole movie theater is at the very top and in the very middle," Ms. Livingston said. "But you have to get here early enough to snag it." Then she turned around and walked away, disappearing into the crowded lobby before Jonie had a chance to say thanks.

When Jonie and Brandon walked into the theater, Jonie looked up into the crowd. The previews had already begun, and she was having a hard time finding two seats together. As they climbed the stairs toward the top, her eyes scanned the middle of the top row; it was already filled up, just as Ms. Livingston had predicted. Finally, just as the movie's opening credits began to play, they found two seats together in the third row.

Chapter 9

At precisely noon on Monday, Alice walked up to Meredith sitting at her desk in the small waiting area outside of Jerry's office. Meredith wore a hot pink blazer-and-skirt set and greeted her with a smile.

"Good morning. My name is Alice Livingston. I have an appointment."

"Yes..." Meredith looked at the brown leather-bound planner on her desk and ran her bright pink nail down the page until it reached today's date.

"There you are!" she said cheerfully. "Mr. London will be—"

The door to Jerry's office flew open and he rushed out.

"Alice!" Jerry adjusted his tie and shrugged on his jacket. He glanced at his watch before extending his right hand.

"I'm so sorry to have kept you waiting. Meredith, why didn't you tell me Alice was here?"

"Actually, sir, she just—"

"I just got here, Jerry. I don't have much time. This really shouldn't take long."

Jerry nodded and looked at Meredith. "Hold my calls until this meeting is over."

"I always do that when you're in a meeting."

Alice saw Jerry scowl at her, and she felt a flicker of sympathy.

"Come on in," Jerry said, holding open the office door. "Would you like something to drink? Coffee?"

"No, thank you."

"Please, have a seat." Jerry gestured toward the large leather chair centered in front of his desk.

Jerry's office was exactly as Alice had expected: a lot of mahogany and leather. Behind him hung a painted family portrait of him as a boy, with his parents standing stoically behind him. The portrait captured their everyday faces perfectly: his parents serious, Jerry grinning. She had to admit, he certainly hadn't inherited their lack of personality.

Jerry sat behind his desk, adjusting his tie again, clearing his throat, and pressing his fingers together in a prayer position. Alice found it unsettling.

"What can I help you with today, Alice?"

She cleared her throat.

"You've been visiting the pool for many years, Jerry, measuring my interest in selling. How long...twenty years?"

"Probably so." Jerry leaned back in his chair and glanced at the ceiling as he calculated in his head.

"The precise number doesn't matter," Alice said. "Your father was the same. He came by often when I was a kid. God rest his soul. My father appreciated his persistence, even though he was never interested in the offer."

"It must be hereditary," Jerry said, trying for a smile. Alice didn't return it.

Alice looked around, wanting to make this quick. She was used to seeing Jerry at the pool, where she could politely signal he needed to leave. Here, she was in his domain.

"My reason for coming here today is to address your offer. I understand it...the positives, the negatives, the freedom it could give me."

Jerry nodded, anticipating her next words.

Alice leaned forward, clutching her purse. "But I do not accept your offer. And I will never accept it, Jerry. Please, do not come by the pool anymore to talk about this."

Jerry flinched slightly, opening his mouth, then closing it. Alice continued: "You're welcome at the pool anytime as a paying guest, but do not show up asking to buy it. If you do..."

Alice paused.

"Well, please, Jerry, just don't."

Alice stood and held out her hand. Jerry lifted his slowly, suspending it in mid-air until Alice leaned closer and grasped it. His hand was soft and sweaty, not what she expected.

"Goodbye, Jerry." Alice walked out of the office and gently closed the door behind her.

~

For Jonie, the next weeks were a blur. If she wasn't at work, she was with Brandon. Since their first date, they had become inseparable. They spent their breaks trying to hold hands without Ms. Livingston seeing them. They knew she wouldn't like such fraternizing at work.

On their days off, Brandon came over to Jonie's house and ate dinner with her family, then they tossed a Frisbee in the backyard or watched a movie with her parents. Sometimes they walked around the mall with their friends.

One morning as Allen dropped Jonie off at work, he asked if Brandon was joining them for dinner that night.

"Gosh, Dad! I think you like Brandon more than I do. Maybe *you* should date him."

Allen smiled weakly as he put the car in park.

"But to answer your question, no, he isn't supposed to come for dinner," Jonie said.

"Okay, good. Let's have dinner tonight, just the three of us."

"Sure, whatever, Dad."

That evening, Nancy made lemon pepper chicken, one of her specialties, along with French-style green beans and scalloped potatoes. She even made apple pie for dessert, and Jonie wondered what the special occasion was.

Judging by the way her parents were acting, though, it seemed as if the special occasion was a funeral. They hadn't really spoken two words to her since she'd gotten home from work.

At first, she was afraid she'd done something to make them mad, but as she thought back over the past few weeks, she couldn't think of anything terrible that she'd done. In fact, she'd been spending so much time with Brandon that she'd hardly spent any time with just her parents, like she used to.

Oh, wait, she thought suddenly. *Am I going to get a lecture about spending too much time with Brandon? Are they going to make me break up with him?!* She started to sweat, and just like that, the delicious dinner on the table made her feel sick to her stomach.

"Potatoes?" Allen asked. Jonie looked down at her empty plate.

"Sure," she said, her mouth dry.

A few moments passed before anyone spoke. Then her dad broke the silence.

"Good dinner, honey." He pointed his fork at his plate for emphasis. "Very good."

"Thank you, dear," Nancy answered, a tight smile on her face.

"Okay guys." Jonie decided she'd had enough. She put her fork down on the bamboo placemat. "What's going on? You two are weirder than normal this evening."

Nancy looked at her husband and ever-so-slightly shook her head. Allen put down his fork and smiled softly at his wife and then at Jonie.

Suddenly, Jonie felt a sensation of *déjà vu*. She remembered having been in this situation before, and she recalled the looks on their faces the last time they had this conversation.

At first, she was relieved when she realized that they weren't asking her to break up with Brandon But that relief didn't last long because she knew what her father was about to say. Something he'd said to her many times before.

"Jonie, I found out last week that there's a job available elsewhere, and it's a good job. It's guaranteed for at least three years."

Allen paused for a moment, watching Jonie.

"I have to take it. It's too good of an opportunity to pass up."

It took Jonie a few seconds to get her mouth to actually open. It had gone completely dry, and her tongue stuck to the roof of her mouth. She had a hard time swallowing. Finally, she found her voice.

"But I thought your job in this town was guaranteed to last three years." Jonie looked at her mother for backup, hoping that she also remembered him saying that. "What happened?" She heard the sharp edge in her voice, but she didn't care.

"That's what I was told at the time," Allen said wearily.

"Where is this new job? Why can't Mom and I stay here and you can stay in a motel during the week like you've done before, and then come home on the weekends?"

"We can't do that this time," Nancy said. Jonie noticed that her mother looked tired. "The new job is in Tennessee."

"Tennessee?! That's so far away!"

"We'll live in a little town called Springfield," her mother continued. "It's about twenty miles from Nashville. You'll love Nashville, Jonie, it's a big city with a lot of things to do. There are a few colleges there, too."

"College?" Jonie said, scooting her chair back and looking at her mother. "How can you even think about college? I'm just now getting ready to start my junior year of high school."

Nancy looked at her husband, who cleared his throat.

"Speaking of that. We don't think it would be a good idea for you to start your school year here and then just have to leave a few weeks later."

Jonie stared at him in silence.

"School in Springfield starts in three weeks. So we'll need to move in about two weeks."

Jonie couldn't believe what she was hearing.

"What about my job at the park pool?"

"What about it?" Allen said. He took off his glasses and rubbed his eyes. Jonie could tell he was exhausted and already tired of her questions, but Jonie didn't care. It didn't seem like anyone in her family cared about her life and her happiness, so why should she care about theirs?

"Well, it sounds like I won't get to finish out the season. I made a promise that I'd be there the whole summer."

"I know," Allen said softly. "But if you really look at it, Jonie, you're only going to miss a week or two of work. Because you'll be starting school anyway. And then the pool closes after Labor Day, right?"

"I was going to work the weekends until Labor Day," Jonie mumbled, although she knew it didn't matter what she said. It seemed as if her parents had made this decision without caring how it would affect her.

"Jonie, sweetie, we're really sorry about this," Nancy said. "We're not exactly thrilled either. We like this town, we've made friends, too."

At that moment, Jonie didn't care about her parents and their friends. All she cared about was that she had to leave the job she loved and the boy that she really, really liked.

"And I bet you can still stay friends with Brandon," her dad said, his voice filled with forced enthusiasm. "You can still talk on the phone and write letters."

Jonie had held back her tears, but at the sound of Brandon's name, her eyes welled up and the tears began to stream down her face. Allen looked uncomfortably at his wife.

"Jonie, I'm sorry sweetie," Nancy said. "Would you like to go to your room? You can take your plate up there if you'd like. It's okay." She smiled at her daughter and squeezed her arm.

Jonie couldn't speak. Instead, she just nodded and took her plate to the kitchen. She'd barely touched anything, but she wasn't hungry.

She slowly climbed the stairs to her bedroom, closing the door behind her. She didn't have the energy to do anything else besides crawl under the covers and cry herself to sleep.

~

The next day, Jonie stood outside Twin Pines Lodge, the air heavy with the scent of pine needles. When she woke up that morning, she hadn't planned to come here. But when her mom asked her how she wanted to spend the day, this is where she heard herself ask to be dropped off for a while. Her mom seemed to understand, promising to return in a few hours.

In her pocket was a folded bright green sheet of paper. She'd picked it up from the lodge check-in desk a few weeks ago when she had walked up there on her lunch break to look around the gift shop. It was titled "Twin Pines Summer Programs: Environmental Education for All Ages," and she'd noticed one listing called "Creek Critters" that had sounded kind of fun. The sheet said to meet in the lodge lobby at ten, and already a small group had started to form.

She'd thought about inviting Jennifer to come with her. Last night, she called her and told her the big news. While Jennifer had been upset and couldn't believe Jonie's parents were doing this to her, which is what Jonie needed last night, today she woke up realizing she just wanted to be alone to clear her mind and figure out a plan. And to be around people who weren't talking about U-Haul rentals or real estate listings in Tennessee.

The heavy lodge doors opened and shut as families bustled in and out: a mom buying postcards in the gift shop, a couple asking for trail maps, two kids arguing about who got the last root beer in the vending machine.

A man in khaki shorts, hiking boots, and a hunter green polo stepped in front of the small group and introduced himself as Ranger Matt. Jonie adjusted the straps of her backpack and, along with the others, followed him outside and up a small hill behind the lodge.

After a few minutes, Ranger Matt stopped at the trailhead and stood in front of everyone with a clipboard in hand.

"Welcome to our Creek Critters adventure!" He smiled and looked over the group. "We'll be hiking down to Little Bear Creek today. It's shallow and safe, but just a heads up, your shoes might get a little wet."

A few kids giggled. One dad groaned about ruining his sneakers.

Ranger Matt continued. "We'll be looking for insects and small creatures that live in the water and other animals that help us tell how healthy our stream is. Salamanders, frogs, maybe a crayfish or two if we're lucky."

He handed out small nets, magnifying lenses, and clear cups. "If you find anything, let me know, and we can identify it together."

Jonie hung near the back as they started down the trail. The sunlight filtered through the canopy in shifting, dappled patches, warming her shoulders. She could hear the creek before she saw it, and despite how frustrated she was feeling, she couldn't help but smile a little.

Around her, people chatted easily. A teenage boy teased his little sister for being scared of bugs. An older woman talked about how her husband used to bring her here in the seventies. A young couple took turns pointing out mushrooms.

Jonie kept quiet, trailing behind, thinking about the words her dad said: "We'll need to move in about two weeks."

The trail opened into a clearing where the creek curved wide and shallow, the sun glinting off the ripples. Ranger Matt set down a backpack and motioned everyone closer.

"This is one of our cleanest streams in the park," he said proudly. "You can see the pebbles at the bottom. That means the oxygen levels are high, and there's not much pollution. If you ever visit a stream and it's murky or has algae coating everything, that's not a good sign."

He knelt, scooped up a handful of water, and let it trickle through his fingers. "Crystal clear. That's what we like to see."

Jonie crouched by the bank, letting the cool water lap against her hands.

A little girl next to her dipped a net into the water and squealed, "I caught something!"

"Let's see," her mom said. "Oh, yeah! Look at that little guy."

Ranger Matt walked over, leaned down, and smiled. "That's a mayfly nymph. See those three little tails? They only live in really clean water. Good find!"

The girl grinned, holding up her net like she'd won a medal. Other kids peered at the critter through the mesh before wandering away to find their own.

Jonie smiled faintly and turned back to her own patch of water. She moved a few stones aside and swirled her net. When she lifted it out, a tiny crayfish scuttled across the mesh. Its shell was the color of rust, claws snapping at the air.

"Hey, nice catch!" Ranger Matt said as he walked over. "That's a young crayfish, probably just a few months old."

Jonie watched it crawl across her hand before she gently set it back in the water.

As the group explored, Ranger Matt pointed out other details: how the roots of sycamores kept the soil from washing away, how dragonflies were a sign of clean water, and how frogs could tell you a lot about the environment's health.

"Nature has a way of adapting, even when things change fast. It finds new balance."

At first Jonie wasn't sure if Ranger Matt was talking about the creek critters or her.

A breeze rustled through the leaves, carrying the scent of damp moss and wildflowers. Jonie sat on a flat rock at the edge of the water, her shoes soaked but her mind a little quieter.

She thought about everything she'd planned for the rest of her summer and the next few years. Even though she wanted to go to college far away, like California, she'd come back home to Twin Pines to work every summer. Maybe she'd even learn to swim well enough to become a lifeguard. She always thought that one day Brandon could teach her.

Jonie smiled at the thought, and she blinked to fight back the tears that were starting to well up. Maybe they could make it work long distance. They could write each other letters, send postcards, and talk on the phone. By next summer, she'd save up enough to buy a car. She could drive to New York every summer and stay with Brandon's family.

It all sounded possible in Jonie's head, the kind of hopeful, half-formed plan that teenagers make when they can't imagine losing the world they know. She wanted to hold onto the smell of chlorine and sunscreen, the feel of the sun on the grass underneath her feet, and the piercing whistles of the lifeguards slicing through the air.

Jonie picked up a flat stone and flicked it across the creek. It skipped three times before it sank.

About an hour later, when the program wrapped up, the ranger gathered everyone. "Thanks for joining me this afternoon. We hope you had fun, and remember, the smallest creatures can tell you the biggest stories about an ecosystem."

Some people began to drift toward the trail that led back to Twin Pines Lodge. Kids compared their bug finds, and couples posed for pictures with the creek behind them. Jonie lingered, taking a deep breath. For the first time since hearing her family's news, she didn't feel angry or trapped. She had a plan. Maybe she'd have to start over in Tennessee, but maybe not everything had to end.

Chapter 10

The next day, Jonie arrived at work a little early. She'd asked her dad to drop her off fifteen minutes ahead of schedule so she could find Ms. Livingston and share the big news sooner rather than later.

Allen didn't mind. In fact, he was just glad to see his daughter in a better mood than she'd been the other night after dinner. He hated seeing his daughter cry, especially when he was the reason.

"Have a good day," he said as he pulled up to the front of the pool. Jonie smiled weakly and grabbed her bag from the back seat.

Ms. Livingston's office door was closed, but that didn't mean she wasn't in. Jonie had learned to spot the faint glow of light under the door, something she'd picked up on quickly as her assistant. She took a deep breath and released it slowly before knocking softly three times.

"Yes?" Ms. Livingston's voice sounded cautious.

"Good morning, it's Jonie."

"Come in!"

Jonie pushed open the door and let it close behind her. She placed her bag in one of the chairs across from Ms. Livingston's desk and sat down heavily in the other. Without realizing it, Jonie let out a huge sigh as she settled in her seat.

"Well, goodness." Ms. Livingston looked at Jonie curiously. "It's a little early for you to be here. What's going on?"

Jonie felt a lump in her throat and was instantly mad at herself. She had gone to bed feeling a little better about things. But when she woke up, she had that sinking feeling in the pit of her stomach, as if she was hearing the news from her parents all over again.

"I have something to tell you." Jonie spoke carefully over the lump in her throat. "My dad's job is making him move, and so that's what we're doing. We have to move and we're doing it in two weeks."

Ms. Livingston laid down her pencil and sat back in her chair. She looked at Jonie without saying anything.

"I'm really sorry because it means that I won't get to finish out the summer working here, and I know I said I would, and I feel so bad about that." The words flew out of Jonie's mouth. She thought that if she could get them out quickly, she could keep from crying. Her efforts proved futile as tears began to run down her cheeks.

Ms. Livingston, who still hadn't spoken a word, opened a drawer and handed her a few tissues. Jonie tried to say thank you but instead just nodded as she tried to stop her sobs. She thought it was weird that Ms. Livingston continued to sit in silence. But she also knew that if she had asked her anything, she wouldn't have been able to answer.

Finally, Jonie pulled herself together. She sat up straight and looked at Ms. Livingston, who was staring down at her hands folded on her desk.

"We're moving in two weeks," Jonie repeated. "So I can start school on time at the new place."

"That makes sense."

Jonie blew her nose again. *A little sympathy would be nice*, she thought. An awkward silence fell on the room before Ms. Livingston spoke.

"Where is your family moving?

Jonie realized that with all of her crying, she hadn't given Ms. Livingston many details.

"We're moving to a small town that's really close to Nashville, Tennessee. I can't remember what it's called. Springfork, Springview, something like that."

"Nashville is a nice city," Ms. Livingston said. "A lot bigger than Olmstead, that's for sure."

"Yeah, that's what my mom said, too. We'll see, I guess." Jonie looked up at Ms. Livingston. "Have you ever been?"

"Yes, a long time ago."

"What's it like?" Jonie perked up ever so slightly. "Neither of my parents have been."

"It's big with a lot of things to do. Restaurants, museums, and of course all kinds of music." Ms. Livingston smiled softly, as if she was remembering something.

The clock on the wall suddenly caught Jonie's attention.

"Yikes, it's almost time to meet," she said, noticing it was nearing time for the morning huddle. She was really just thankful for a reason to leave. "Thanks for letting me cry in your office. And for the tissues."

Ms. Livingston was quiet. Jonie waited for her to say something like, "You're welcome" or "We'll miss you around here" or "You still have two weeks, let's enjoy the time you have left here." Or even a "You owe me a box of tissues."

But Ms. Livingston said nothing. Instead, she stood up from her desk and grabbed the clipboard laying on the shelf next to the door. She locked the office behind them, and walked alone toward the gazebo.

~

Later that afternoon, Alice did something she hardly ever did: she left the pool around noon and walked up the hill to Twin Pines Lodge. Normally she packed her lunch or grabbed something quick from the concession stand between tasks, but today she wanted a change of scenery.

The air conditioning hit her as soon as she walked inside the lodge. Park visitors were lined up at the registration desk, and she had to squeeze by families to get to the stairs.

The restaurant wasn't as busy; a few families lingered over sandwiches, and a couple of hikers were putting in an order. From the second-story view inside the restaurant, the lake sparkled like diamonds.

Sally spotted her almost immediately. "Well, hey there, stranger," she said, smiling as she walked over with a menu tucked under her arm. "I didn't expect to see you up here in the middle of the day."

"I needed a break from the chlorine." Alice managed a small smile. "And maybe a grilled cheese sandwich."

Sally grinned. "You've come to the right place. Sit wherever you want."

Alice grabbed a table by the windows. From there, she could see the edge of the pool in the distance, just a shimmer of blue through the trees.

In her mind, she could still picture Jonie's face from earlier that morning, full of heartbreak as she talked about her family moving away, yet again.

Alice knew exactly how Jonie was feeling, and that was precisely why she had chosen to simply listen. She'd lived it herself: the endless cycle of moving and saying goodbye, of pretending it didn't matter because crying never helped.

Sally returned with a tall glass of water and a lemon wedge floating at the top. "Do you want fries or chips with that sandwich?"

"Fries," Alice answered without a second thought.

Sally jotted it down, then lingered at Alice's table for a few seconds.

"You know, I haven't seen Jerry London around much lately. He used to come in all the time for his usual turkey club with extra pickles. I haven't seen him in weeks."

Alice looked up, startled by the mention of Jerry's name. She took a sip of her water, the ice clinking softly.

Sally smiled, half teasing. "Well, I guess that's good, right? That's what you said you wanted."

Alice gave a faint shrug. "Maybe."

But it didn't feel good. That was the strange part. She'd spent so long resenting Jerry's smug grin. She thought hearing that he'd disappeared from one of his usual haunts might bring her some satisfaction. Instead, it just made her feel nothing. Or maybe a little sad, if she was truly being honest.

When Sally walked away, Alice rested her chin on her hand and looked out the window again. A couple of kids chased each other across the lodge lawn, their laughter echoing faintly.

She thought about Jonie.

Ever since she'd met her, Alice had seen so much of herself in her: that mixture of independence and need for friends, of wanting to belong somewhere but never being quite sure if she did. She'd let herself believe, for reasons she didn't quite understand, that maybe Jonie's family would end up staying in Olmstead the way hers had. That this town might give Jonie the kind of roots it had taken Alice years to find.

Her sandwich arrived, golden and crisp, but she didn't have much of an appetite anymore. She picked at the fries, watching the way the sunlight shifted across the dining room floor.

Poor kid, she thought. It wasn't just Jonie's loss; it was her parents', too. Alice knew how hard it was for families like theirs, moving from job to job, chasing the next contract. Her own parents had hated uprooting her so often. When her father found Olmstead, he'd sworn it would be the last move. He'd poured everything he had into that crazy dream of building a swimming pool at Twin Pines. And that dream had somehow turned into her own legacy.

Now Alice found herself wishing Jonie's mom or dad would come up with some wild idea of their own, something that would make it possible for them to stay.

She sighed, brushing a crumb from the table. The restaurant buzzed softly with conversation, but Alice felt miles away.

~

Later that day, Jonie's stomach twisted as she thought about telling Brandon the news. She'd felt a little better after coming up with a plan, a fragile, hopeful plan that kept them together somehow. It involved summer breaks at the park, handwritten letters, and maybe even college someday.

But still, she knew this conversation was going to change everything.

They were on their lunch break, sitting together as they always did. Ever since the second or third week of summer, lunch had become their thing: just the two of them usually, side by side under the faded striped umbrella near the shallow end.

Today, a handful of kids shrieked as they splashed around in the water. Sunlight bounced off the surface and flickered across Brandon's face like tiny flashes of glass.

While Jonie tried to eat, Brandon kept reaching for her hand, brushing his fingers over hers until she finally stopped pulling away. He grinned as he laced their fingers together. With her free hand, she tried to hold her sandwich steady, but it felt ridiculous, trying to act normal when her heart was pounding this hard.

"You've got a funny look on your face," Brandon said, squinting at her.

"Yeah..." Jonie's eyes drifted toward a pair of twins splashing near the ladder. They wore identical swim trunks, and between the two of them, four bright-orange floaties bobbed in the water like pumpkins. Brandon followed her gaze.

"Those kids are fine. World's best lifeguard is right here," he teased. "So what's up? You seem super distracted."

Jonie took a breath. "There's something I need to tell you."

Brandon's grin softened. "Okay. Shoot."

Jonie planted her bare feet on the warm concrete and turned to face Brandon. Her palms felt damp against her knees as she met his eyes.

Brandon mirrored her movement, sitting up straight. He smiled in that easy, familiar way that always made her chest tighten. "You're making this sound serious," he said, placing his hands lightly over hers.

Jonie cleared her throat. "My parents told me the other night that we're moving. In like, two weeks."

"You're moving houses? Did they finally find a bigger one?"

She blinked, confused, and then remembered what she'd told him earlier in the summer. About how their place was tiny and that her parents were supposed to find a bigger house. She remembered exaggerating, saying that in the new house, she would have a bathroom all to herself.

Brandon was still smiling. "And before your dad even asks, yeah, I'll help you move. Just make sure there's pizza."

Jonie's throat burned and she stood, taking a few quick steps away before turning to face him again.

"We're not just moving houses," she said quietly. "We're moving towns. My dad got a new job in Tennessee. We're leaving in two weeks."

Brandon's smile faded, his mouth parting slightly. "Please tell me you're joking."

She shook her head. "I wish I was. It sucks. I hate it. I thought moving here was supposed to be it. I actually like this town."

Tears stung her eyes and then overflowed, hot and sudden. Brandon stared at his feet, at the scuffed concrete between his toes.

"Yeah," he said softly. "This totally sucks."

"But," Jonie sniffled, wiping off her cheeks. "I have a plan. Kind of."

Brandon's eyes lifted, a curious look on his face. "Let's hear it. And did you tell Ms. Livingston yet? She's going to be so bummed. You're her favorite."

"I am not." Jonie's voice sounded higher pitched than usual. She sighed. "But yeah, I told her this morning before work."

"What'd she say?"

"It was weird." Jonie settled back into her chair. "I expected her to be mad or sad or something. But she didn't react at all. It was like I told her I bought a new shirt or something."

She frowned, remembering the flat look on Ms. Livingston's face.

"She acted as if..." Jonie hesitated, the words forming slowly. "As if she didn't care." Saying it out loud made her stomach twist.

"That's strange." Brandon scratched at a mosquito bite on his ankle. "So what's this plan of yours?"

But Jonie wasn't really listening. Her eyes drifted toward the concession stand, where she knew Ms. Livingston was probably doing inventory.

"I've worked my butt off for her all summer," she said. "Stayed late, skipped lunch. Half the time I was here before she was. You'd think she could at least pretend to care."

"Yeah," Brandon said lightly. "That's rude."

"Do you even *know* how many times I've stayed late?"

"Uh, five or six?"

"Way more. At least once a week since I started. I'm a hard worker."

"I know. Jonie Boloney's the hardest worker at Twin Pines." Brandon reached for her hand again. "Now tell me this big plan."

Jonie hesitated, then smiled faintly. She shook her head a little, as if she was trying to clear her mind and focus on Brandon.

"Right. I move to Nashville—or whatever the stupid city is actually called—and go to school there. We can write letters, talk on the phone, maybe even use that internet chat thing called ICQ. I don't have a computer yet, but you do, right?"

"Yeah, but my sister hogs it."

"Then during the summers, I'll come back here and work at the pool. Ms. Livingston said I'd always have a job if I wanted it."

Brandon nodded thoughtfully. "All right, but where would you stay?"

"At your house." When he didn't respond right away, Jonie pressed. "What do you think?"

A grin slowly broke across his face. "I think it's a great idea." He jumped up from his chair. "We've got that extra room upstairs. It gets kind of hot, but we've got fans."

Jonie laughed for the first time that day. "I'll make it work."

Then his expression shifted. "What if Ms. Livingston doesn't want you back next summer? Or what if you don't want to make the drive? How far is it, anyway?"

"I don't know. I'll have to check a map at the library."

Brandon shrugged. "If you can't come back, maybe I'll go to Tennessee. Get a job there in the summer. What's the town called again?"

"Springfield. But I'm telling people Nashville. It sounds cooler."

"Nashville it is," Brandon said with a grin.

Out of the corner of her eye, Jonie saw Ms. Livingston step out from behind the concession stand, scanning the pool deck.

"Uh-oh. We better go," she whispered. "She's looking over here."

As Brandon walked away toward his lifeguard chair, Jonie looked at him and hoped, with everything in her, that maybe her plan wasn't just a plan. Maybe it could be real.

~

After work, Alice walked home to find that her refrigerator was bare. She couldn't even have a bowl of cereal because she was out of milk. The pool had been so busy the past several days that she hadn't had time to shop.

She sighed. What she really wanted to do was crawl into bed. Instead, she decided to drive the ten minutes to Palmer's Market and grab just a few things.

As she drove through the park, she admired the couples strolling hand in hand along the paths and the families finishing up their kayaking adventures on Twin Pines Lake. She stopped in the middle of the road to let a mother deer and her two fawns make their way across. As she waited, she started to feel warm and rolled down her window.

"That's better," Alice said aloud as the evening breeze hit her face.

Palmer's Market was crowded, and she somehow felt even more tired since she'd left her cabin. She just wanted to get in and out as quickly as possible.

As she moved through the produce section, Alice looked toward the bakery and caught a glimpse of a familiar person disappearing around the corner. His short legs moved quickly, and Alice would have recognized his plaid driver hat anywhere.

Jerry was the last person Alice wanted to see right now, despite the fact that she had been thinking about him lately. Not that she'd ever admit that to anyone, especially Sally, who insisted on updating her every time he did or didn't have lunch at Twin Pines Restaurant.

Alice kept her eyes fixed on the rows of canned vegetables as she hurried her cart past the endcap display. She could feel the awkward heat in her cheeks. She'd caught sight of him just in time and had immediately pivoted her cart and gone the opposite direction.

If Alice was being honest with herself, she wasn't even sure why she was avoiding Jerry. She had the upper hand in their relationship, and she'd set a boundary she'd been wanting to for years.

She turned down the cereal aisle, rubbing her forehead with the back of her hand. The fluorescent lights seemed especially bright today. Her vision shimmered around the edges.

Probably didn't eat enough today, she thought.

She grabbed a box of instant oatmeal and then walked a few steps and reached for tea bags, the next item on her list. But when she took a single step forward, the aisle tilted. The shelves seemed to stretch and sway like they were underwater.

Alice blinked hard. Her hand shot out to steady herself on the edge of the cart.

Just breathe. It'll pass, she thought, even though her stomach was seized by panic.

But it didn't pass. A wave of dizziness washed over her, stronger this time. The floor felt unsteady beneath her feet, as if it was sliding sideways. A rush of heat swept through her body. Her ears filled with a low hum.

"Oh," Alice whispered, though she wasn't sure if she actually made a sound. The last thing she saw was the rows of tea blurring into one another.

A few moments later, she woke to a gentle voice nearby.

"Alice? Alice, hey—come on now, open your eyes."

Her eyelids felt heavy, and she forced them to lift. The ceiling lights glowed above her, but the brightness was gentler now, shadowed by someone kneeling beside her.

Jerry leaned over, one hand braced against the floor, the other hovering uncertainly near her shoulder. His face was drawn with concern, eyes wide and focused completely on her.

"You fainted," he said softly. "Scared the hell out of me."

Alice blinked again, trying to sit up. Jerry immediately supported her as she sat up and leaned against the shelf.

"I—I'm fine."

"You weren't." Jerry's voice cracked ever so slightly. "You went straight down. I saw you turn into this aisle and figured, well, honestly I figured you were trying to avoid me, but then you just... collapsed."

He swallowed, looking almost embarrassed by the admission.

"I ran over as fast as I could. I thought..." His jaw tightened. "I thought something serious had happened."

Alice stared at him. She'd known Jerry for years, but she had never seen this look on his face: worry. Genuine, unfiltered worry.

"Jerry," she said quietly, feeling overcome with emotion. "You didn't have to—"

"Yes, I did." His voice was firm. "Of course I did."

For a moment, neither of them spoke. The hum of the grocery store went on around them. A few curious shoppers hovered farther down the aisle, but Jerry ignored them completely, his attention fixed on her.

"You shouldn't be alone right now," he said sternly. "Let me walk you somewhere to sit. Or do you want me to call someone?"

Alice shook her head. "No. No, it's just low iron. I'll be alright. I just need a minute."

He nodded, but his eyes didn't leave her face.

"Okay. Then I'll sit with you until you feel steady again."

"Jerry, I don't want to be a bother—"

"You're never a bother."

Something in Alice's chest tightened. She felt suddenly exposed, vulnerable in a way she never allowed herself to be. She looked away briefly and then back at him.

"Thank you," she said quietly, and the words felt heavier than they should have.

Jerry gave her a soft, relieved smile.

"Of course, Alice. That's what friends do."

Chapter 11

Jonie couldn't believe how quickly two weeks flew by. She had tried her best to savor every moment: her last days working at Twin Pines, conversations with Brandon and Jennifer, and even time spent in her house, which she couldn't believe she had once thought was tiny. Now she regretted not appreciating its coziness.

One evening after work, Jonie went with Brandon to his dad's hardware store, where he helped to load bags of mulch into a customer's pickup truck. Jonie wandered around the small shop with its tightly packed aisles, picking up and putting down tools she had never seen before and parts that she had no idea what they were for.

Once Brandon finished helping his dad, he and Jonie wandered outside, the chime above the front door ringing loudly. Up and down Chestnut Street, downtown businesses were hopping.

Red and white lights from Art's Drive-In Diner five blocks away glowed against the dusky sky, and music drifted faintly from somewhere down the block. A few people sat outside Scoops Up ice cream shop, their laughter carrying on the evening air.

They walked quietly for a few blocks, their shoulders brushing now and then. Brandon picked up a small rock and tossed it lazily into the gutter before saying, "It's hard to believe we're almost done with the summer."

"It feels like it just started," Jonie replied.

He nodded, kicking another rock. "This morning my mom told me I needed to start thinking about college, since I just have two years of high school left."

Jonie smiled, looking up at the streetlights just flickering on.

"She's totally right! We should apply to schools somewhere with mountains or beaches. Like California or Colorado." She looked excitedly at Brandon.

He chuckled. "I thought you liked it here?"

"I love it here. You know that. But there's such a big world out there. I want to see new places before I come back here, and college is the perfect time for that." Brandon didn't reply.

They stopped in front of The Tilted Raccoon souvenir shop, its windows crammed with postcards, magnets, and Twin Pines State Park t-shirts. The hot pink fluorescent "open" sign flickered, and Brandon pulled on the door.

"Come on. We have to get you something before you run off to Nashville."

The shop smelled faintly of cedar. Jonie trailed her fingers over the displays: mini snow globes with tiny bears inside, pine-scented candles, mugs with chipmunks, owls, and cartoon fishermen.

Brandon picked up a mug and held it out to her. It had a cartoon bear lounging in an inner tube with sunglasses on. Above it, in bold letters, it read: Bearly Surviving Twin Pines State Park.

Jonie laughed. "That's ridiculous."

"That's why you need it." Brandon handed it to her. "And you can take a marker and write 'swimming pool' on it."

When they reached the counter, Brandon paid before Jonie could argue. "My treat. A going-away gift."

Jonie traced the rim of the mug with her finger as they stepped back outside. The air had cooled, the sky fading into a navy blue. They started walking again, slower this time. Jonie looked over at Brandon, still thinking about their earlier conversation.

"What about you? You ever think about going somewhere far away?"

Brandon shrugged. "Not really. I always figured I'd go to the community college over in Owenton. It's close, and they've got a decent business program."

"Business, huh? I thought you'd go for something outdoorsy."

He grinned. "Nah. My dad keeps saying someone's got to take over the hardware store one day. I figure if I get a degree, I'll be ready for that. Maybe even expand it a little."

Jonie glanced at him. "I bet there's a college out in California with a decent business program."

"Maybe." Brandon's eyebrows furrowed. "That's so far away, though."

Jonie smiled faintly, looking down at the mug in her hands before she placed it gently into her purse.

"Yeah. It is." Her voice came out quieter than she intended. A week ago, Brandon had been so excited about their plans for the future. She didn't realize that his idea of "going off to college" was just driving to the next town over.

Jonie felt a heaviness in her heart and tried her best to shake it off. She had enough to worry about: the move and a new school, just to name a few.

Suddenly her thoughts filled with something Ms. Livingston had said to her during one of her first weeks at the park pool, when she'd become overwhelmed during a hectic birthday party: *Take a breath. Then start again. One thing at a time.*

She just wanted to focus on the fact that tonight would be the last time she and Brandon would see each other outside of work for a while; months, maybe longer. The next day, her dad would pick up the moving van and they would spend two days packing. Then, early in the morning, too early for Jonie to even contemplate now, the Kirkland family would pile into the van, with Buttercup the Buick firmly attached to the tow, and head to Tennessee. Classes at Jonie's new high school would start a week later.

Everything was changing so fast. Jonie didn't like it one bit. She took a deep breath and slowly let it out as they continued walking.

As they approached Main Street, the sounds reached them well before the lights did: music floating on warm summer air, laughter, and the hum of rides spinning. When they rounded the corner by Casella's Bakery, Jonie stopped in her tracks.

The Olmstead Summer Carnival stretched along the entire downtown square, spilling across the closed-off streets in a blur of motion. Strings of lights looped from booth to booth, and the smell of fried dough and kettle corn drifted all around. Jonie's eyes were wide as kids darted past them with glow sticks, and a band played on stage in front of the courthouse.

"Oh wow! I forgot today was the start of the summer carnival! I thought I was going to miss it."

She and Brandon blended into the crowd. Someone handed them paper tickets for rides, and one of Brandon's basketball teammates waved from inside the ring toss booth.

Jonie continued to feel a nagging inside her, reminding her that everything she did tonight was the last time she'd do it. Maybe for a long time, maybe ever. Jonie noticed that Brandon wasn't talking much. She wondered if he was trying to make it last; if he was counting down these moments the same way she was.

They passed the funnel cake stand, and the sugar scent made her stomach flutter. Brandon bought her a lemonade, the kind in the big plastic cup with a smiling lemon printed on the front. Jonie held it between both hands as they wandered.

Rounding a corner, her eyes lit up as the Ferris wheel came into view, lit in soft blue and white lights, turning slow and steady against the dusky sky. Brandon followed her gaze.

"That one?" he asked.

"That one."

They stood in line, swaying slightly to the sounds of the Aerosmith cover band. When it was their turn to board the Ferris wheel, the carnival worker opened the metal gate, and they climbed into a seat together. The bar locked across their laps with a soft clank.

The wheel lifted, and the sounds of the carnival grew softer, like the world was drifting away beneath them. As they went higher, they could see the whole town: the rooflines, the brick buildings, the hazy outline of the pine-covered hills of Twin Pines State Park in the distance

"This is nice," Jonie said, her voice barely audible above the hum of the motor.

Brandon smiled and gently squeezed her knee as the Ferris wheel paused near the top, the metal carriage rocking gently in the warm breeze.

Jonie pressed her hand against the metal of the seat, trying to memorize everything: the view, the breeze, the feeling of being suspended over her summer, over her whole world.

She looked at Brandon. The carnival lights reflected in his bright brown eyes. He smiled at her, that crooked smile that made her chest ache in the best way.

"It's hard to believe this is our last date before you…" He trailed off.

"I know," she whispered.

Brandon didn't finish the sentence, and Jonie didn't want him to.

Will I ever feel like this again? she thought.

So she leaned her head on Brandon's shoulder. The wheel began moving again, carrying them down through warm air and carnival music. For tonight, she was just a girl riding a Ferris wheel with the boy she liked in a small town that finally felt like home.

As they reached the bottom, Brandon laced his fingers through hers.

"Let's go again," he said. And Jonie nodded and smiled.

~

The next morning, Jonie woke up with a headache and a feeling of dread in the pit of her stomach. It had jerked her awake from a deep sleep two hours before her alarm was supposed to go off. After that, there was no going back to sleep. Jonie hadn't felt like this since last semester when she had studied for hours for an algebra final and woke up feeling like she hadn't studied at all.

Even though she and Brandon had made a plan, Jonie still worried, especially after their conversation last night. She'd moved before and left friends behind, and even though they kept in touch for a while, it always ended. For once, she really, *really* didn't want her friendships to end. Not with Jennifer or Brandon. And she wasn't worried about Jennifer.

An hour later, Allen gingerly pulled into the parking lot of Twin Pines pool. Since that first day he brought Jonie, he had figured out how to pull his car in and out of the gravel parking lot without scraping the bottom.

"Guess we won't have to worry about Buttercup hurting herself anymore."

Jonie looked at her father and smiled weakly, and he smiled back at her, a sad and understanding look behind his glasses.

"I'm sorry, Jonie. I know how much you liked this place. I was hoping this might be it for us. I really did."

"I know, Dad."

"But sometimes in life, you just can't pass things up. Even if it's the harder choice." Jonie looked at her watch. She needed to go.

"You'll see one day," Allen added softly.

Once inside, Jonie walked toward the pool, which was still and glassy, reflecting the pale sky. She kicked off her sneakers and sat down on the edge, dangling her feet in the cool water.

She thought about Brandon's words again, how he'd said this town was where he wanted to stay and how sure he'd sounded. Jonie admired his steadiness. And even though she wanted to call this town and this park her home, she didn't want to miss out on exploring other places.

She couldn't imagine standing still. Not yet.

A soft breeze rippled across the water. In a few hours, kids would be splashing and laughing, and Brandon and his friends would be perched in their lifeguard chairs. But for now, it was just her, the water, and the soft hum of a summer that was almost over.

Jonie was shaken from her thoughts by a gentle hand on her shoulder. She turned her head to the left, and Brandon smiled down at her.

"Good morning, Jonie Baloney."

Before they had a chance to talk, Ms. Livingston's voice on the intercom snapped Jonie and Brandon to attention, and they followed everyone else over to the gazebo for the morning huddle. Even though

Jonie had been working at the park pool for four months, she still felt as if she needed to be on her best behavior around her boss.

Nothing had changed with Ms. Livingston all summer, and Jonie had tried to explain it to Brandon and Jennifer: one minute you felt like you were her star pupil, and the very next minute, it felt as if she didn't have any patience for you. Brandon had only shrugged his shoulders.

"I've never, ever for a single moment felt like I was that woman's star pupil."

"Good morning, everyone," Ms. Livingston said. "Today is going to be busy. As all of you know it's the last day of…"

Jonie felt her heart skip a beat. Her face turned red in anticipation of what she knew was about to happen, and her ears rang so loudly she was sure she wouldn't even be able to hear Ms. Livingston.

"It's the last day of the season for daycare centers to bring their large groups of kids," Ms. Livingston continued. "So let's keep up the good work so that they'll all want to come back next year."

Half of the staff members groaned while the other half clapped weakly. Jonie could barely hear any of it because her heart was beating so loudly in her ears.

Once Jonie calmed down, disappointment washed over her. She had told herself that she didn't want Ms. Livingston to make a public spectacle of her last day and talk about how awesome she was in front of everyone.

When it didn't happen, though, Jonie realized that she had actually wanted it more than anything.

For the next ten minutes, she stood in between Brandon and Jennifer, listening to Ms. Livingston talk about concessions and overtime and the upcoming closing of the pool for the season. She listened really closely, hanging on every word so that she would hear her name when Ms. Livingston said it.

But Jonie waited all the way until everyone was dismissed, and she never heard it, not even once.

~

Late that afternoon, Alice stood near the pool's edge, observing everything around her. Happy kids splashed in the water while their parents relaxed in lounge chairs.

The last days of summer always felt different, like the air itself knew something was ending. The pool was quieter than usual today. It always was this time of the year as families started devoting more of their free time to getting ready to start the new school year.

For the past month, Alice had woken with a light anxiety tiptoeing across her body, creeping from her hair to her fingertips, settling into her heart by the time she drank coffee and performed her morning meditations. She was worried about the pool winding down for the season, and she was worried about her health.

Then she fainted in Palmer's Market and had immediately booked an appointment with her doctor.

But today, she felt okay, almost like herself. She closed her eyes for a moment, taking in the faint buzz of cicadas in the nearby trees. She detected movement beside her, and suddenly Jonie appeared.

"Ms. Livingston, my dad is here. I just wanted to say goodbye."

Alice smiled and took a deep breath before looking at Jonie.

"I'll see you next summer, right?"

"You bet!" Jonie's eyes brightened with surprise, and then she paused before continuing.

"I also wanted to thank you..." Her eyes began to turn red, and Alice wished she had a tissue to give her.

"Thank you for giving me my first real job," Jonie said, with a catch in her voice. "I really love this place."

She lifted her hands and looked around. "I felt like I belonged here.

Alice held her arms out and smiled gently. Jonie immediately embraced her in a hug.

"You do belong here," Alice said after several moments. "You will *always* belong here."

After Jonie disappeared through the turnstile and into the parking lot, Alice looked out across the pool, its surface calm. She and her parents had built this place for others to find a piece of themselves in it. Maybe, someday, it would belong to someone who loved it in just the same way.

Epilogue
from That First Summer: Part Two

The sound of a fire truck blared from the nightstand. Jonie groaned and grabbed her phone to quiet the incessant noise. She made a mental note for the one hundredth time to change the sound of her alarm.

"Just ten more minutes." She buried herself deeper under the covers.

But it was no use. Less than a minute later, Jonie heard the creaking of her bedroom door, and before she could turn over, three little bodies jumped into the bed and threw themselves all over her.

"Mommy! Mommy!" The tiny voices sang in unison. "Wake up!"

Jonie peered out from under her white down blanket and smiled at the three sets of eyes staring expectantly at her.

"Get out of my room!" Jonie grumbled dramatically, and two kids erupted in giggles. Joey, the youngest, was six years old, and he followed his sisters Gretchen and Laney everywhere they went.

"Mommy, Laney and Joey are hungry," announced Gretchen, the eldest. Even though Gretchen was only nine, she'd assumed responsibility for her younger siblings. She liked to gather the consensus of the group and then relay that back to Jonie, just as she was doing now about breakfast.

"Are you hungry, too, Gretchy?" When Gretchen nodded and smiled, Jonie reached up and squeezed her cheek.

"Okay, let's go." As soon as Jonie said that, the three little ones jumped off of her just as quickly as they had pounced. She swung her legs over the side of the bed, firmly planting her feet inside the fuzzy, teddy-bear shaped slippers the kids had chosen as her Christmas present a few years ago.

~

That evening, before Jonie had a chance to close the front door, her kids ran toward her with their arms open wide. She bent down on one knee and let them come to her, her arms wrapping around them all at once. Then just as quickly, they ran back into the kitchen where they continued their homework.

Jonie groaned as she slowly stood up. She was forty-one years old, and her knees sure felt like it.

"Hi, Mrs. Taylor." The grandmotherly woman sitting at the kitchen table sipped a mug of steaming tea and smiled gently.

"We're just finishing up our homework," Mrs. Taylor smiled. "I'll get out of your hair." She always said that as she was preparing to leave.

Jonie had hit the lottery when it came to neighbors. After her divorce, she and the kids moved into an apartment complex across town. Mrs. Taylor had not only welcomed them into the neighborhood, but she had grown close to them, becoming Jonie's after-school babysitter.

In exchange, Mrs. Taylor only asked that she occasionally get some of Jonie's incredible cooking.

"Thank you so much again. Oh wait, before you go, I made you something." Jonie walked over to the refrigerator and opened the freezer door. She pulled out a glass Pyrex container with a red lid. Jonie loved those dishes; they had been her parents.

"What is it this time?" Mrs. Taylor said excitedly.

"It's a new recipe that I tried out. It's a lasagna, but instead of using those wide flat noodles, you use vegetables like eggplant and squash."

Jonie handed the dish to Mrs. Taylor, who inspected it with a skeptical look.

"If you don't like it, just let me know, and we won't use that recipe again." She winked at her elderly neighbor.

"Thank you, dear." As Mrs. Taylor opened the front door and readied herself to shut it behind her, she turned around.

"Honey, I put your mail on the coffee table. The kitchen counter was just too cluttered."

Later that evening, after the kids had gotten their baths and were tucked into bed, Jonie made herself a mug of tea. As she kicked off her shoes, her eyes moved to the pile of today's mail on the coffee table. She'd forgotten all about it.

"What's this?" She held up a large, flat manila envelope with her name and address on it. Jonie looked at the top left corner.

"Jerry London," she read aloud. "I don't know a Jerry London."

Then her gaze moved below Jerry's name to the city and state hand-written beneath it: Olmstead, New York.

Jonie's breath caught in her throat.

Fighting the urge to rip the envelope open, she instead carefully unsealed the flap with her manicured nail and peered inside as if something might bite her.

She slowly pulled out a single type-written piece of paper addressed to "Ms. Jonie Kirkland." She found it interesting that this Jerry guy knew she was divorced; it hadn't been finalized that long.

Dear Ms. Kirkland,

I am sorry to inform you of the passing of Alice Marie Livingston on August 22, 2025. As her legal representative, I am informing you that in her last will and testament, Ms. Livingston named you a beneficiary of her estate. Please call me directly at the phone number above to discuss. If I do not hear from you within 30 days of the date of this letter, I will again attempt to contact you.

I am sorry for your loss. Ms. Livingston was an important part of the community.

Sincerely,

Jerry London, Esquire

Jonie's heart raced.

For the next twenty minutes, she picked up the letter and re-read it at least ten times. She turned it over, examined its font, and even smelled it, trying to somehow see if it could be a joke.

Finally, still speechless and confused, she simply put the letter back into its envelope. She turned the lights off in the living room, peeked in on the kids, and then climbed into bed.

But Jonie didn't sleep a wink that night

Stay in touch

Thank you so much for reading! I truly hope you enjoyed this book. **Please take thirty seconds to leave a star rating on Amazon.** This is the best way to support independent authors.

If you'd like to stay in touch, sign up for **the Enchanted Mountains newsletter** at eleanorromanybooks.com to learn about new releases and upcoming events and to get subscriber-only extras!

Best,
Eleanor

About the author

Eleanor Romany is a romance author who believes in starlit kisses, long hikes through the woods, and the power of a good love story.

The ENCHANTED MOUNTAINS series is a love letter to Allegany State Park (ASP) in Western New York, the place where she, her husband, and his family vacation each summer. For the past 70 years, her husband's family has spent a week each summer at ASP, biking, swimming, fishing, kayaking, and hiking through its majestic landscape.

It's also the place where, deep in the forest along Eastwood Meadows Hiking Trail, her husband asked her to marry him, and she said yes.

When Eleanor isn't writing sweet, feel-good novellas set in the Enchanted Mountains, she's reading, checking out new restaurants, or daydreaming about her next fictional couple. She writes from somewhere cozy and quiet, and she always roots for happy endings.

For more information, visit eleanorromanybooks.com and follow her on Instagram at @eleanorromanywrites.

About the series

The ENCHANTED MOUNTAINS series from Eleanor Romany is a heartwarming collection of stand-alone romances set in the scenic beauty of fictional Twin Pines State Park.

While the heart of the series is the majesty of nature, the true stories are to be found within the characters. The books follow the lives of the people who come to the park all year long seeking peace, adventure, or escape and those who make up the Twin Pines community looking for the same things.

From chance encounters and second chances to late-night walks under starlit skies, love always finds a way in the Enchanted Mountains.

9 798999 679611